SPINNING INTO OBLIVION

SPINNING INTO OBLIVION

SANTHOSH GANGADHARAN

PARTRIDGE
A Penguin Random House Company

ISBN:	Hardcover	978-1-4828-4895-3
	Softcover	978-1-4828-4894-6
	eBook	978-1-4828-4893-9

Print information available on the last page.

To order additional copies of this book, contact
Partridge India
000 800 10062 62
orders.india@partridgepublishing.com

www.partridgepublishing.com/india

CONTENTS

This novel, my first real attempt to create one, is a mixture of my experiences and imagination.

I wanted to pursue my dreams. But I felt the dreams were pursuing me always.

I dedicate this maiden venture to the ever-loving memories of TK, Bhargu, RG, and Ponnu.

The Dreams You Make

The German scientist August Kekule got the idea of the benzene ring from a daydream of a snake chasing its own tail. This seemingly unrelated vision thus laid the foundation for one of the most basic concepts of chemistry: aromatic compounds.

It is all history now. But the scientist pursued his dream to create the benzene ring, and several compounds followed.

It is important that one takes a cue from one's dreams and follows the lead to reach a conclusion.

Whether the conscious mind had created a dream and planted it in the subconscious mind or the subconscious mind picked up the dream do not matter. One has to go ahead to achieve the desired result.

It can happen. The subconscious mind can give you great ideas during your sleep, and when you wake up, if you are able to recall what you had seen in your dream, maybe you can pursue the route of your dream to its roots.

Normally, most of the dreams you see during your sleep, you tend to forget them when you wake up. But definitely it will be in your mind the moment you wake up, and if you try to recall the dream sequence at that time, you might be able to remember the whole thing. But if you do not make an effort to remember immediately after you wake up, the dream goes into oblivion.

That is where Kekule was able to do better than a normal person; he kept recalling what his dreams were, and he pursued the dreams.

I had had many wild dreams which one may think cannot happen. How these got implanted in my subconscious mind, I have no idea. They say that what you are thinking before you go to sleep may appear in your dreams. But some of the dreams which I had seen, I had never thought of in my conscious state.

From my childhood days, I used to dream about very large airships invading the sky and fighting with the people on earth. Those were days much before the *Star Wars* movie was produced by Hollywood. In those days, I had never seen any books or movies which could have given me any idea about these types of airships attacking from the sky.

The sky would be filled with fleets of airships. These airships would be so huge like our aircraft carrier vessels. They would start firing and bombing in clear visibility. There would be no one on earth who could retaliate against these attacks, and the people would run helter-skelter. I would run for cover and find shelter under some big boulders or so. The dreams would never go beyond this. I do not remember whether I had ever seen how the attacks started or from where these airships came.

Now I think, if I had given more thoughts to these dreams, I could have done something connected to these attacks. Not that I was good enough to carry out some research to design airships of similar kind, but I could have written some fiction involving such airships. Maybe *Star Wars* could have been based on my story if I had the patience to pursue my dreams. But I never followed up on these dreams, and they had always remained as dreams.

Another dream I used to see was of me jumping from one place to another, similar to kangaroos. With extra effort given on my feet to pump them up, I would be able to move around like a rubber ball.

I should have persisted in pursuing this possibility of humans jumping great distances like Hanuman, the monkey god in Hindu mythology. I see movies from the Orient where the martial arts specialists are able to move in a fashion similar to what I'd seen in my dreams. Those people had their dreams, and they made it into reality through movies and photographic tricks.

That brings me to my latest dream, and this was what made me at least pen up a few things from my thought processes. Call it a fallout of the 'better late than never' theory.

It was on the night of 9 August 2010.

I had slept earlier than usual and got up just after midnight. I had to drink some water, and this dream was coming up fresh in my memory. I could recollect what I had seen in my subconscious mind during that short sleep.

I was able to move with my beloved ones who were no more with us, the precious departed souls of our dear and near ones. I was virtually with them and moving in the air with them, a travel during which I was able to speak to them and feel them. I could feel the elation in me over this remarkable achievement, and I could understand that I was able to make this happen by moving myself at very high speeds within the atmosphere of earth.

At the peak of the high-speed movement, I was able to turn into a bodiless mass similar to those of the souls prowling around our biosphere. Many of them were around, and I was able to meet a number of people known to me—like my father, mother, uncles, and aunts—during this awesome episode.

Can this really be made possible? I don't know what made me think like this and put this notion into my mind. While awake, I had never thought of such possibilities, but while sleeping, somebody had implanted this into my mind.

So can I not pursue my dream? There is a thin thread of imagination. Am I strong enough to convert this thin piece of imagination into a strong plot to make a novel or a movie or maybe push myself into the unknown depths of life after death.

No, I should not say *life after death*. It should be termed *life after life*. If one can prove this concept, one is no longer dying. But it will be like losing one life to start another life—the eternal life of life after life!

CHAPTER 1

Noetic Science

The second consecutive day it happened to me, I was getting up in the middle of the night with some strange dream still lingering in my subconscious mind.

I tried hard to remember the dream. It was just at the edge of my mind, but not coming out to the conscious state. That was a very bad feeling to have, like not being able to vomit when you really want to vomit or not being able to sneeze when you are about to sneeze.

It brought a lump in my throat, and I felt as though I was getting suffocated. But I knew there was a dream and that it was something similar to the previous night's dream. It was not anything scary, but it was something which made me wake up in the middle of the night.

I tried to remember what I was doing just before going to sleep. I had been reading Dan Brown's *The Lost Symbol*. It was a fascinating novel. The author had taken great pains to go in depth about noetic science.

The concept behind noetic science is admirable. One's own thought energy could be utilized to make superhuman efforts by concentrating. Having a number of people concentrating together on a single object could work wonders.

Was the dream somehow connected to the novel that I was reading? Could be.

Normally, they say that what you have been doing before going to sleep will affect your subconscious mind.

Last time I met Dr Lakshmi, she had explained the psychology behind dreams. She could explain things in a simple manner. Actually, psychology is such a complicated matter. But Lakshmi is so talented and involved in her subject she becomes animated when she starts talking about anything connected to her doctoral thesis. That is why she is able to convey her views so easily.

What I could understand from my chat with her was that the things with which you get emotionally involved will design your dreams.

That used to always make me wonder whether you should pursue the dreams you see or the dreams pursue you to its end.

Either way, dreams are a matter of never-ending interest. If you start to think of it, you go deeper and deeper in search of the bottom of this huge well.

Going back to noetic science, I could recall what Dan Brown was talking about in the book. Fascinated by the explanation given by the author, I had searched the website to get to know more about this latest wing of science.

The Institute of Noetic Science says, 'Noetic Sciences are exploration into the nature and potentials of consciousness using multiple ways of knowing—including intuition, feeling, reason, and the senses. Noetic Science explores the inner cosmos of the mind—consciousness, soul spirit—and how it relates to the outer cosmos of the physical world.'

They research into the mind–body interaction, consciousness, the paranormal, alternative and complementary healing, subtle energy, information imprinting, the human body field, and other aspects of nature and human biology that were routinely dismissed by conventional science.

Basically, they give more importance to the power of the mind or the energy that can be created by one's own mind. This could be used with good intent of its own keeper or could be streamlined for the benefit of others. By our own concentration, we are able to create energy and make it flow from our minds to other objects outside us.

It is a matter of consciousness which gives us power, but this power is latent in your subconscious mind. Since it is not a normal method, the word *paranormal* is used, and that word creates a sense of abnormality to the listener. The ordinary human being would think of it as a crazy idea and dismiss it summarily.

But that was not the way to look at it. With the kind of dreams I had, I could sense a connection between what I read and what I felt in the dream.

Was I man enough to make my thought energy do some small things at least? Could I generate enough concentration to make this happen? But if it did, it could be a powerful support for humanity. One had to use it with good intentions.

By then I was convinced that my dream had connections to the concept of noetic science, which I had picked up from Dan Brown's novel.

So the previous night's dream could have been an offshoot of the lost symbols of noetic science. But what about the dream I had before that?

CHAPTER 2

The Hadron Collider

I remember that I had got up from my sleep in the middle of the night. I had a feeling of travelling at a very high speed. That had nothing to do with Dan Brown. It would be more appropriate to connect the speed with Jason Bourne.

The movies about Bourne could have given me an effect of running at a high speed. In the movie, the hero had been running most of the time, and continuous watching of the movie really could have affected my equilibrium.

But I had watched the movie a long time back, and there was no chance of that making any impact now unless it had been embedded in my subconscious mind so well.

I had a feeling it was not Jason Bourne who had affected my mind the previous day. It was something else moving at high velocity. My eyes wandered around the room and then focused on the table. Yesterday's newspaper was lying there. Was there something which had captured my mind while reading the newspaper?

On an impulse, I took the paper and sifted through the pages. There it was—the Hadron Collider experiment being conducted in Switzerland. The scientists had succeeded in creating boson by allowing two atoms travelling at supersonic velocities in opposite directions to collide.

The report very explicitly detailed the experiment and gave the reader an effect of the high-speed travel.

The Large Hadron Collider (LHC) allowed scientists to reproduce the conditions that existed within a billionth of a second after the Big Bang. That was the time the universe started with a bang, creating energy and matter.

My eyes wandered over the paragraphs. A lot of stuff related to science had been written in the article. But what captured my attention was the mention of antimatter. I kept reading on this.

> The Big Bang created equal amounts of matter and antimatter, but we only see matter now. What happened to the antimatter?
>
> Every fundamental matter particle has an antimatter partner but with opposite properties such as electric charge. The negative electron has a positive antimatter partner called the Positron. Equal amounts of matter and antimatter were created in Big Bang, but antimatter then disappeared. So what happened to it? Experiments have already shown that some matter particles decay at different rates from their antiparticles, which could explain this. One of the LHC experiment studies these subtle differences between matter and antimatter particles.

I thought about these facts about matter and antimatter. That could have been what was on my mind and could have triggered my dream about speed and its consequences. LHC allows particles to travel at high speeds and collide to form that very particle which matters most—the antimatter.

My mind could have been working on the effects of a Large Hadron Collider within the realm of a dream and was producing an atmosphere conducive to the generation of antimatter.

I looked at the article and resumed reading.

> Why do some particles have mass while others don't? What makes this difference?
>
> Particles of light, known as photons, have no mass. Matter particles such as electrons and quarks do have mass and we are not sure why. British scientist Peter Higgs proposed the existence of a field, the Higg's field, which pervades the entire universe and interacts with some particles and this gives them mass. If the theory is right then the field should reveal itself as a particle, the Higg's particle. The discovery of a Higgs-like particle was announced on 4th July 2012 by the ATLAS and CMS teams.

These scientists were out to prove the reasons for some particles having mass. Those particles, like photons, are massless, and they do travel very fast, covering millions of miles. Those particles travelling at very high speeds would have a status of weightlessness and not *masslessness*. But how does one create masslessness for a particle having mass in its present existence?

My dreams could have been connected to these kinds of thoughts, which had been planted in my subconscious mind by the article I had been reading the previous night.

The clock on the wall announced that the time was already seven, and I now had to rush to get dressed up to reach my office in time. When the thoughts of my office invaded my mind, they erased all other thoughts for the time being. Now I had only one intention. I had to reach office in time and should not be late for the morning meeting with engineers.

CHAPTER 3

Inception

A week passed without any further incidence of that curious dream. I'd had normal days and nights, and my routine life continued monotonously.

Then it struck again. I wouldn't say I was terror-struck, but that odd feeling came again on that early Friday morning. Similar to earlier incidents, this time also it was around two or three in the morning.

I could feel the presence of something or somebody else beside me. Even though it was in the dream, I could sense it even when I got up, sweating profusely. This time I tried to remember what I did or see in the dream. It was pretty difficult to get it out of my subconscious mind. But I knew it again had something to do with speed and spinning. It was as though somebody was trying to plant an idea in my mind. What could be this unseen force, or what was this idea being put in my mind? That was something I couldn't recollect at all.

The more I thought of it, the more it was passing into oblivion. I tried to think very hard, and that brought in the customary effect of falling asleep. Soon I was fast asleep.

Friday morning was always a bit lazy, with it being the weekly day off in Oman and other GCC (Gulf Cooperation Council) countries.

I was in the drawing room, switching on the TV, when my eyes fell on the CD lying on the table. That was the movie

I had seen last night—*Inception*. It was a very good movie and fast-moving. The basic concept of the movie was fantastic—planting an idea into another man's mind while he is asleep and later forcing him to carry out actions to achieve that idea.

Then it came to me—that was almost the same thing which was happening to me in my previous day's dream. The effect was similar. But what was happening to me was in some way different. I was sure my dream had nothing to do with the present. It was something connecting the past with the future.

The movie had showed the story of a dream within a dream and how people managed to implant a dream into the mind of a person. They tried to achieve what they want to achieve in the real world by manipulating the dreamer in his dream world. Whenever they wanted the dreamer to stop dreaming, they would give him a kick to stop dreaming so that they reaped the benefit of what they had created during the dream.

It was a rather complicated movie, and I could not understand the full concept behind the whole story. But the implantation of the dream in the subconscious mind was something I could grasp, and that was what stuck in my mind.

It is hard to believe the concept of inception, but anything can be made possible by the strong mind of a person working on the weak mind of another person.

Just imagine how Hitler had managed his people in carrying out only what he wanted them to do by infusing fear into all persons around him. Many of the dictators in the history of the world had used the same technique to their own benefit. But they all succumbed to their own strategy, and when it came to facing the same situation, they became lambs.

The plot in the movie was fantastic. The movie could have influenced my mind, planting a crazy notion, whatever it was, into my mind.

I sat on the sofa, sipping my morning tea. I allowed myself the luxury of having all this space only to myself and having all the time in the world to relax and sip my tea—no other botheration at the moment. That gave me enough time and inclination to put together the parts of the dreams I had been having these days.

The first time, I was affected by the concept of noetic science—creating high energy from one's own thoughts. I had the feeling that there was somebody else who was thinking like me, and the two thought energies were combining together to create some sort of message or plan for the future.

The second incident was connecting the past and the future with the effects of high speed. I could get the feeling of something going round and round at a very high speed, like a yo-yo being spun by a child. This was merging into a feeling of nothingness or zero-gravity levitation. But even when I was in a status of nothingness, I got a feeling of some other formless entity close to me. What could this be?

The experiment with the Hadron Collider had clearly affected my mind, giving me the thrust at high speed. The scientists were finding out the effect of collision at high speed to create the smallest dot of everything that matters close to nothingness. If you think of things in this world and those which may exist in the other world as matter, the world of life after life could be termed as antimatter. That means maybe the materials or matter in our world could turn into nothingness at very high speeds, and it may collide with the nothingness created from things at high speed from the other world.

It could be seen as a positive factor tending towards zero and another negative factor also tending towards zero, which will enable them to meet at that zero point. Could this happen?

My dream the day before clearly indicated that somebody else was trying to influence my mind through the dream by planting his or her ideas. Were all these aspects interrelated? Or were they just the work of fantasy toying with a confused mind?

Noetic science, Hadron Collider, and *Inception* were together crushing my mind into a pulp. If I did not take it seriously, it would further torment me in the coming days since more of it would not make any sense to me any more. But if I tried to analyze these thoughts emanating from my dreams, maybe I could come to some sort of conclusion and happily call it my theory of spinning into oblivion.

I decided to pursue my theory to get myself enlightened in a field which was till now alien to me.

CHAPTER 4

The Spook of Mary Roach

I had been reading Frederick Forsyth these days. My son, Viv, had inculcated the love for Forsyth in me.

Viv was an ardent reader. He would read anything from fiction to literary works. He had a good collection of books back at home. I used to think that if he had not gone for engineering, he would have turned up to be an author.

Recently when I went to India, I had brought with me a number of books from Viv's collection.

I had just finished one of many and was returning the book into the box where I kept all novels I've already read. As usual, I went through the titles of books I had finished reading. Then I noticed *Spook* by Mary Roach. I had read it sometime back.

On an impulse, I took the book and returned to the drawing room.

After the bout of dreams last week, I had been sleeping comparatively better nowadays. It was as though the sequence had ceased to appear in my mind. But still I had a feeling that I was seeing something related to those dreams even though it was not becoming evident.

I used to always get a feeling of being close to somebody during the day after I had seen that person in my dreams the previous night. This was invariably true. Sometimes when I had been able to recollect a part of a dream where I had seen a certain person, that feeling of closeness to that person would follow me in my waking hours the day after.

These days I had been thinking more of my parents who were no more with us. I see them every day in the photos hung in front of our bed, along with those of my wife's parents. All four of them had been so dear to us, and we remember them every day.

I had a gut feeling that the closeness towards them that I was getting could be due to my sighting them in my dreams. Could there be some relation to meeting them and the movement at high speed which I was experiencing? I so dearly wished to find out the connection.

Spook by Mary Roach was lying in front of me. Mary Roach was a supporter of the concept of life after life. She had been searching for the truth of the afterlife and the status of one's soul after death. She had been going to a great extent to find out the fact for herself. She, very avidly, was expecting the afterlife to be true.

My dreams, Roach's life after life, the feeling of closeness to my parents—with all these put together, a chill went up my spine. Rarely had I experienced goose pimples, but now my arms were filled with them.

That was it. I had been talking to my parents in my dreams. That was the explanation I got when all these facts were put together.

I tried to analyse these thoughts further.

The spinning at high speeds was taking me to some other field—might be like Higgs's field of antimatter. There the matter would be able to meet with the antimatter. Maybe my parents, in their life after life, were the antimatter with whom my subconscious mind was seeking to interact.

In my dream, I had been spinning very fast and reaching a state of nothingness to be taken into the world of antimatter, which was a variant of nothingness.

My mind was on fire.

I took the cup of tea in front of me and started to sip slowly to douse the fire within me. I had to think rationally. All these thoughts seemed to be irrational.

I should allow myself to be logical before my thoughts went astray into the wilderness of mystical living.

My eyes again took in *Spook*. If Mary Roach could think and write about the rationality of life after life, why should I not search a bit more to prove that my theory of spinning into oblivion was true? If that was true and the Hadron experiment proved the antimatter to be existent, why not interrelate them to reach a point of contact with the souls around us?

This way of thinking elated me since that could enable contact with our lost beloved ones. Rather than finding the rationality behind such thinking, it was better to ensure that it was logical.

I would think more of it to make myself conclude that it was logical.

I closed my eyes for a while. I must have drifted into a slumber. I was seeing my mother near me, touching my ankle in a bid to wake me up. That was the way she had always done it. She pushed my ankle a couple of times, and I woke up with a start.

I could clearly remember my mother standing next to me and could still feel the touch of her wet hand on my ankle exactly where I had seen her touching me in my dream.

Again a chill ran through my spine.

CHAPTER 5

Dubai Dunes Safari

Almost five months had passed, and another new year had dawned. I had totally forgotten about those incredible dreams I had. It was time for my wife and daughter to make their biyearly visits to Dubai.

I was at Muscat Airport, waiting for their plane to land. The airport, although not so big as Dubai's, was always fascinating to me. This was where my pursuit for a career outside India started.

Mostly something good was going to happen to me when I come to this airport—either I was going home to my loved ones or my loved ones were coming to be with me. Both were things to enjoy in the middle of hectic office work and travel. I would rather forget the trips to the airport for sending off the visitors.

The arrival area was bubbling with lots of people from different parts of the world. These days the airport had become so crowded. No wonder the airport authority had gone ahead with the construction of a new airport terminal with 104 check-in counters and 48 aerobridges. Within three years, this dream of Omanis would become a reality.

There they were, my Jai and Kav. It had almost been six months since their last trip to Oman. Pushing the trolley through the crowd, we went out to the parking lot. Soon we were on the way back to Sohar, a drive in the night for close to two hours.

Their favourite pizza, thin and crispy exotica, was already in their hands, and they started devouring it with relish. I too had a piece of the exotica. All said and done, the Pizza Hut in Sohar made beautiful pizzas; even our Italian visitors had vouched for the same. So without fail, I would carry a large pizza whenever I go to pick them up from the airport. The culmination of a three-hour flight and a two-hour car drive was always the tasty pizza.

While stuffing her mouth with a bite of pizza, Kav was talking about the flight. Then suddenly she changed the subject to the impending trip to Dubai.

'Dad, this time we want to go for the desert safari. We should experience this at least once.'

I had never been an advocate of such crazy adventures. 'No, Kav. Why should we take such risks like the dune-bashing? Anything can happen while driving over those sand dunes. There had been instances of the SUV overturning.'

She was insistent. 'Dad, don't be a sissy. Even Uncle Sur and Aunty Suv had taken the ride with our other cousins in Dubai. Nothing happened to them. They enjoyed it. So why don't we also do the same?'

I was totally opposed to this idea. But when the argument started to get heated, my wife joined in, siding with Kav. So finally, I had to give up since it was a democratic decision of two against one.

We decided to do the daring drive in the dunes.

After two days, we were on our way to Dubai. We stayed at our usual haven, ZiQoo, the Japanese hotel apartments in the Discovery Gardens.

I had the phone numbers of several desert safari organisers. Finally, we settled with a Pakistani tour operator with a

Hummer. Kav and Jai were thrilled to ride in a Hummer for the first time. The photo of the Hummer was relayed immediately to my son in America through WhatsApp.

In the afternoon that day, we were with Yousef, the organizer and driver of the Hummer. He had been doing similar trips for the last twelve years and now had become one of the leaders of the team of desert drivers. He was also part of rescue teams in the desert. These words gave us enough courage to make the drive.

We had three teenaged lads from Kuwait as companions. The first stop was at Safari Centre, which was on the way from Lahbab to Madam, the next town in the Emirate of Sharjah. The small shopping centre offered small-time buys and eatables.

The highlight of the stopover was the peacock, which took a fancy towards Kav. I snapped some quick photos of Kav sitting very close to the beautiful peacock. As if to entice us, the peacock started its dance with its pretty feathers fully spread out. That was a scene to behold.

Soon Yousef called us back to the Hummer. He had leaked out some of the air from all four tyres. We could understand from him that for the drive over the sands, the tyres should not be fully blown up.

The drive over the sand dunes started. I had the privilege of sitting right in front by Yousef's side. Others were in the seats behind us.

In the beginning, the drive was nice and enjoyable. But very soon we had to change our mind about the comfort of the ride. The car started bouncing off the sand dunes while it made steep climbs over the sand. The uncertainty of what lay in front was eating up our minds, and soon our enthusiasm gave way to tension and then to panic.

Even though Yousef had twelve years' experience in these deserts, the terrain changes every now and then, with the dunes taking different shapes as dictated by the desert winds. So what you see today would be alien to what you will see tomorrow. To make matters worse, there were a number of SUVs running helter-skelter all over the place. Any two could collide at any time if one of the navigators is not so adept.

Then it happened. Yousef went up fast on a sand dune. When he reached the top, he realized that the other side was a sheer fall with absolutely no slope. The ace driver turned the car to the left to avoid the fall just by seconds and inches. The back-seaters would not have felt any difference since they were not seeing what was in front. The full impact of the danger was on my mind, and my heart virtually skipped a beat. I had visions of many who had departed before me from this world. A sense of great panic enveloped me. Could something go wrong?

Yousef could not care less. He just veered off the vehicle to one side and immediately turned right to descend the slope at an angle.

I almost cried out. I could see a couple of figures moving ahead of us, and I could feel their presence. Some familiarity crossed my mind. Had I seen them before? I wanted to stop Yousef so that this huge vehicle travelling at a high speed would not crush them. But all of a sudden, the shapes went out of sight. Where did they go? The desert was open all around.

Maybe there was nobody. Was my mind fooling me? I tried to recollect what I had seen a few seconds before. Yes, they were right in front of my eyes. But they were only some vague shapes resembling men. I had seen similar forms sometime somewhere, but I could not recall where or when.

But there was no time to think more of it since the vehicle was racing down the slope and all the others were screaming their hearts out.

The vehicle straightened when it reached down where the sand was even in nature. In one voice, all of us chanted, 'That's enough, Yousef. Let us go to the camp.'

We had a feeling of emptiness in the mind, brain, and also the stomach. Yousef agreed to take us to the camp, where better things awaited us.

Through a labyrinth of sandy lanes and then asphalted roads and back to sandy tracks, Yousef took us to the desert camp. The camp was fully lit, with a number of small shops lined along the boundary, and some small huts on another end to accommodate the overnighter.

At the centre was a wooden platform, where the dancers would perform. Behind the dance floor was where the buffet had been arranged.

We settled on a mat with many pillows close to the dance floor. We had heard that they perform beautiful belly dances in these camps. We had not seen such dances before and hence were very eager to see them perform.

Outside the camp, there was a person taking the participants for a camel ride. We too had gone near that to see others ride camels. The camels were really tall. I thought we might get that feeling of sitting on the parapet of a skyscraper while sitting on a camel. So I had already decided not to go on a camel ride.

But Kav was adamant. She wanted to experience the ride. I reminded her of what had happened to her brother when he did a camel ride while we were in a resort with our friends in Delhi. Viv, my son, was small at that time. The camel got up from its sitting posture with Viv clinging on to my friend's wife; both were on top of the camel. What we did not account for was the height of the camel, which was quite high, and the branches of the tree. The camel did not understand anything, and it started to walk. The branches of the tree brushed Viv's tiny face, and he started yelling out loud. The attendant somehow managed to stop the camel and bring the riders down. The pain from the bruises made Viv decide not to try another camel ride in his life.

But Kav was not in a mood to think of what I had told her and had already climbed on to the back of the beast of burden. Another lady, a European, climbed on beside her. The camel Kav was riding went on its way for a round and returned to the same place, with the attendant next to it holding its tether.

Then the camel was sitting down. It bent its forelegs first, and that brought the two ladies on top sliding down to the neck of the camel. Everybody yelled, and more so did the brave ladies. Both hung on to each other while the camel bent its hind legs to make itself level with the ground. Kav jumped down and came running to us. She was panting and was clearly frightened from the slide.

We tried to pacify her, saying it was nothing, that everything was fine. She was telling us it was okay and that nothing had happened to her. She tried to laugh it off. But I could see the terror in her eyes as though she had seen some ghost. I had the feeling that it was not the slide which terrified her. There was something else. But I could not understand what that something was. I did not want to question her further, which would have upset my wife also.

That was what had happened half an hour back, and now we were relaxed on the mat, inclined on the pillows. Jai was as usual intently watching the performers. She was normally a person who enjoyed everything and put her full concentration on what we had come to enjoy. She appreciated everybody's talents and always talked good about what she had seen.

But I noticed that Kav's mind was away from what was happening in front of her. The belly dancers were on the floor, and rhythmic music was on. It was an enjoyable occasion, and those dancers were really artful and sincere to their profession.

I felt hungry, and the aroma of food floating in the air made it even more urgent. I tapped my wife, and she got up along with my daughter. All three of us were famished, and one tap was enough for all to troop towards the common destination. The buffet was a good spread. Two of us were vegetarians and as usual had to search for the food of our liking. But like her brother, Kav ate anything which was tasty and palatable.

Luckily for us, the buffet had both Arabic and Indian dishes. The Arabs eat a lot of green vegetables; there was a good spread of salads along with hummus and *moutabel*, which were pastes of chickpeas and eggplant, and these tasted very good—a pure vegetarian delight.

We filled our plates and went back to the dance floor. The next set of dancers was on the floor, and they were announcing the importance of the dance. They were all men. I thought that this item was going to be dreary after seeing the beauty of the belly dancers. What could these men do to at least come close to the performance done by the preceding dancers, the ladies!

On top of the haunting music, the announcer's voice could be heard in halting English. His accent was typical of such organizers, giving emphasis to the words which he thinks were important for the spectators to recall the text given in their advertisements for the desert safari. Nobody should complain that they did not see what was published on the leaflets.

'The next item will be the tanoura dance of Egypt. This form of dance has its root in the twelfth century. You will find the main dancer in the centre with the other five dancers around him. I am sure you will find this whirling dance enthralling, and it will take you into a different world altogether. With this, I present to you our star performer, Ahmed Mansour, and his team. Enjoy, and I am sure you will love this.'

Then Ahmed Mansour started his tanoura, and my problems too started along with it.

CHAPTER 6

The Tanoura

The music was really enchanting. I could see many of the people gathered around slowly getting up on their feet and swaying to the tune of the music.

The six dancers placed themselves on the dance floor at a set pattern. The main attraction was Ahmed Mansour. He was a lightly built young man. He had the body of a dancer. His face was calm, and his eyes had a peaceful ambience.

Mansour was at the centre, with one dancer behind him and two slightly in front of him on both sides. The other two were almost at the left and right corners. It was a symmetrical formation which gave an impression of a hexagon with the front corner slightly depressed.

All of them wore black overcoats and had flat felt caps covering their heads. They removed the overcoats and put them aside, revealing the long cleaved jacket and the white frock with a black belt at the waist.

They stood holding their arms crosswise, and then they started to move from right to left. As the whirling began, they had their arms outstretched with the hands fully open. The right hand was held towards the sky, and the left hand was opened towards the earth. Their eyes were fixed on their left hand as the whirling picked up speed.

The music and the spinning were so fascinating that I could see most of the spectators moving to the rhythm.

I too was enjoying each moment of their dance, and I could see both my wife and daughter intently watching the dance. They were too engrossed in the events in front of them. I felt happy that I could bring them to see something quite beautiful like this.

Suddenly, I thought I saw a seventh person near Mansour. He was there for a moment and then was gone. But after a few minutes, again the apparition appeared and continued to be there. It was always near Mansour, and thus the formation was losing its symmetry. I could not make out what this person was up to or how he could be allowed to climb the dance floor. He was spoiling the show as far as I thought.

I looked at my wife. She was enjoying the dance. My daughter had a strange expression on her face but was still looking at the dance. I told my wife, 'What is this extra person doing on the floor? He is spoiling the symmetry.'

My wife seemed surprised at what I said. 'What are you talking about? There is no problem in the dance. It must be your eyes. Just keep watching the dance, please.'

I turned my attention towards the dance. But there he was, the seventh guy, and now I could feel that he was trying to pull at Mansour's sleeve as though he wanted Mansour to lose his rhythm. But Mansour seemed to be oblivious to the presence of this seventh man and kept on with his perfect footing.

Soon the whirling came to a stop, and the crowd rose on their feet to applaud the dancers. We were also clapping our hands to the truly magical feat by these Egyptian youngsters.

They performed two more dances with different music, and while dancing, they did a lot of tricks with their frocks and other materials in their hands, like plaques, umbrellas, boxes, and so on. Their years of training enabled them to perform perfectly in front of us. *They were born to entertain*, I thought.

But for me, it was a bit confusing since the seventh guy always seemed to appear whenever Mansour was dancing. This guy disappeared when Mansour stopped dancing. What I could remember was that while Mansour was whirling from right to left, this guy was spinning in the opposite direction, left to right. But he was trying to pull at Mansour. I did not speak about it to Jai or Kav since I knew they had not seen this extra guy over there and would dub me crazy.

Maybe I was crazy. Otherwise, why should I alone have these strange visions?

There was a break for coffee, and we too picked up nice, steaming coffee for ourselves. Seated on the mat while sipping coffee, Jai was talking about the movements of the dancers.

'It was really beautiful. How can they keep rotating without stopping for so much time? I think we would have felt giddy within the first five minutes.'

'I agree with you.' I tagged along with her. 'I had read recently that 10,000 hours of practising any particular activity would make you a master of it. That is why back home, they start training girls to dance from the age of three or five. By the time they reach their teenage years, they would have completed the required amount of 10,000 hours of training.'

Jai nodded her head in appreciation of what I conveyed. But Kav was still silent. She seemed to be lost in her thoughts. What was in her mind? Did she also see the seventh guy just like me?

I cut off my thoughts as the announcer's voice boomed over the loudspeaker. 'Now for the last item on the agenda—the dance of lights. Please do not panic since we will be switching of all lights around us to make you enjoy the show more. Watch and be thrilled.'

The dancers appeared, wearing strange-looking coats. They began their spin along with the music. This time the music was a bit different and was giving an effect of blending with the night sky over us. I could get a sepulchral feeling creeping into me with the music and the appearance of the dancers.

As the whirling took up speed, the lights around us were put off, and then the dancers seemed to go ablaze. Their coats were fitted with a large number of small bulbs of light, and all these were glowing with bright light. The small lamps with the spinning motion gave the impression of the dancers being on fire. It was a superb idea.

I could see that all the people around us were watching the show in total silence. We were being taken into a different world altogether. With the elegance of these young men, the atmosphere had become so enchanting.

And then the seventh guy appeared.

This time the apparition was firmer than in the previous occasions. I think the darkness around Mansour was giving better distinction to the shape of the intruder.

It was clearly trying to disturb Mansour's rhythm. But Mansour seemed to be so preoccupied with his dance that nothing was able to break his concentration. That gave another thought to me—was I the only person seeing the intruder? Was it that Mansour did not see it like I did? That would make me utterly crazy. My mind was clearly playing tricks on me.

I shook my head vigorously to clear it of any effect of blinking. I knew my wife would not approve of my gestures in the midst of so many people. From the corner of my eyes, I could see her looking at me with impatience for a fleeting second, and then she resumed enjoying the dance.

But my daughter was looking back at me from time to time to see what I was doing. I felt she knew what was going on in my mind. But her face showed no signs of understanding, and it wore just a look of concern. Maybe she thought I was not well.

I took my eyes back on to Mansour and his mates. The dance was really wonderful, and the coloured lamps were giving a festive look to the whole dance floor. The crowd was fully immersed in the performance. I thought that I was the only one who was not able to enjoy the concert fully. This seventh guy was presently making my life miserable.

Then for some time, I felt happy. There was no seventh figure, and Mansour was alone in the front, going round and round. Now they started to bring the first layer of lighted frock up, revealing a second set of frock underneath. The first one came out over their heads, and exactly when the frock was covering Mansour's face, the intruder appeared by his side. This time he was trying to push him down, and with the frock blinding him, there was a good chance that Mansour would easily lose his balance.

For a moment, I saw that Mansour faltered. He moved back while still spinning, and in a flash, he took the frock away from his head, throwing it to the side of the dance floor. Once he was free of the frock, he regained full control of himself and went on spinning. The other one kept pace, spinning in the opposite direction.

Soon the show was coming to an end, and the announcer's voice came over the speaker. 'Our performance is concluding now. But before winding up, we have one more item. Any one of you who wants to dance with our great Mansour can come forward on to the floor. You can wear the black cloak and move along with Mansour to the rhythm of the new music. This is one chance to rehearse your dancing talents. But, ladies and gentlemen, please note that those who have problems of nausea, heart ailments, and so on should not try their luck and put us in difficulty. Pregnant ladies are barred from participating. Now come on, my dear friends, and enjoy fully.'

There were only four people who were bold enough to climb on to the floor. I too got up to join Mansour. My aim was to check the seventh guy with Mansour just to get an idea whether he had felt any alien presence.

The moment I got up to climb the floor, my daughter pulled at my shirt. 'Dad, no need. Don't go there now. Better to stay here only.'

I told her, 'No problem, Kav. I will just do a couple of rotations and return. I think I certainly do have that much capacity to dance.' With that, I was walking towards Mansour.

Mansour was looking at me even though there were four others coming towards him. When I was close to him, he said, 'Sir, I think you should not dance. Better listen to your daughter and go back to your seat.'

I was taken aback. How did he hear what Kav had said? She had spoken in a very low voice. Even the nearby people could not have heard her, but this guy at such a distance had heard her. There was something fishy happening.

'Mansour, I just wanted to take a few revolutions with you.' I tried to keep my voice very low. Almost in a hush, I said, 'While you were dancing, I could see somebody else very close to you, trying to push you around. What was that? Did you not see that, or is it that only I had seen it?'

'Sir, I am again pleading with you. Please go back to your seat. Do not come near me or even climb on to the dance floor. It is not good for you.'

'Okay, okay, Mansour. I will just do a few spins and then stop. I just wanted to get a feeling of this excellent method of dancing you have formulated. I bow before you, great artist. The dance was fantastic. I will always remember you.'

'If you insist, it is okay with me, sir. But please go back immediately after two or three minutes. Do not try to hang around, and do not be so curious about anything happening around me. You should forget me after this.'

Another person helped me put on the frock, and then the music started. The five of us began spinning from right to left along with Mansour.

I felt very encouraged with the first few spins. I was good enough to do this. I had thought that I would feel giddy very fast. But no, it was fun. That was when somebody nudged me. I faltered but regained my balance. I was trying to see who had come near me. But there was nobody close enough to have pushed me. So what was it then?

Again there was this push. This time it was harder than the previous one. I lost a few steps and moved towards the edge of the floor. But still I continued. Then came the third push, and I lost control. I fell from the floor and on to the sand around the floor. Luckily, there was good amount of sand, and nobody was standing there.

I could hear people around me crying out in surprise, and many helping hands came towards me to lift me up. People were enquiring whether I was okay, and I shrugged off the initial feeling of embarrassment. Jai and Kav came running to me to take me out of there. They helped me remove the cloak and placed it on the floor.

Meanwhile, they had stopped the music, and the dancing came to an end. I looked up to see Mansour. I very much wanted to talk to him. But he was not to be seen anywhere. He had vanished so fast.

The announcer was telling everyone that the day's program was over and all may leave the place. Those who had night stay passes could stay back to enjoy their hospitality.

We came out of the camp, and Yousef was waiting for us. The three Kuwaiti kids also came running to us. After the incident of my fall, they too decided not to stay overnight.

What started as a joyous ride had ended up a little bit disastrous. I could never have guessed the outcome to be so drastic. I knew one thing—these matters were almost out of my hands. I had to think well before taking any further steps.

We were mostly silent on our way back to the city.

CHAPTER 7

Thoughts Implanted

A spate of pedestrian days ensued. Nothing specific had happened. My wife and daughter had come and gone, and life moved on as usual. I would have to wait another six months or less to have them back again.

I was in the office. Being Thursday, a general lethargy was found all over the office. The impending weekend always brought in the let-me finish-somehow mood on everyone.

I too was at my desk, going through the general emails and deleting many after reading and many others without wasting time to read.

The office boy brought the mail. These days, there was hardly anybody using the post office. Generally, the junk mail only came through the post. Most of it went into the waste bin without being opened. I used to wonder from where the Oman Post generated funds to sustain itself.

But today's mail had a surprise in store for me.

There was a plain envelope with Indian stamps put on it and my address written in a girlish handwriting. I wondered, *Who is this girl or lady who had taken pains to write a letter to me?* Maybe a job application? It couldn't be. People used the email for quicker service. The normal post was considered to be 'monkey' mail by the new generation.

Somebody could have intentionally sent the letter by post so that it did not reach very fast. Maybe the contents were not so important. But I was proved wrong once I opened the envelope.

The letter started with 'My dearest father'. It was from my beloved daughter, Kav. I was taken aback. It was the first time she was writing to me. She used to send birthday greeting cards by post, but never a letter. SMS and WhatsApp messages were being used mainly.

I was very curious to understand the contents and went through the letter.

The things which had been happening without good logic in the last few months had become stranger in nature with this letter. I recalled the day Jai and Kav were leaving Oman to go back to India.

We had not talked about the incident of my falling from the dance floor after coming back from Dubai. Jai had tried to make fun of me on being so clumsy on the dance floor. Kav would look very serious whenever the topic came up, but she never opened her mouth to talk about anything regarding the Dubai dunes safari.

At Muscat Airport, we had finished checking in, and they were about to go inside for immigration check when Kav caught my hand and looked into my eyes. I could see her pleading eyes trying to send a message of caution over to me.

Jai had started to walk towards the entrance to immigration. Then Kav told me, 'Dad, never ever go back to that desert area. That place is not good for us.' With that, she let go of my hand and followed her mother.

Just before vanishing behind the door, she looked back at me and waved. The same pleading expression was there in her eyes.

After that, I had tried to understand what she meant by those parting words. How she could know what had actually happened to me? She seemed to know that something sinister was lurking around that dance floor in the desert. I ought to talk to her when she next came to Oman.

Then I left the matter go and did not urge her to tell me what she knew.

Now she was explaining everything. She knew almost everything, but it had become stranger than before. I started to read the letter once again with more concentration.

> I knew you would not take my words seriously. When I told you not to go back to that place, I really meant that, Dad. I do not want you to go back there. That place bodes evil. There was something there which had pushed you from the dance floor. Others could not see that, but I could see that seventh guy you were mentioning to Mother. I do not know why it appeared only to the two of us. Mother seemed to be oblivious to all those happening around her.

> I strongly feel that there is some unknown hand connecting me to you even though we are miles apart. Somehow I know that you had gone to meet Ahmed Mansour again. That is why I am writing this letter. I did not want to use email lest somebody else sees this. Also, I felt that you should get enough peaceful time to read the letter thoroughly and act wisely.

> It was a couple of months before we came to Oman that it started to happen. Do you remember Aleena, my old classmate from Sohar? She had met me at Oberon Mall one day after she had made a trip to Oman. She specifically called me to meet her, saying she had something to give me. When I met her, she gave me a copy of the

magazine *Thursday* from Oman. The one with your article on the dreams you make.

She had found it interesting, and since you had written it, she wanted to give the magazine to me.

I too found the article quite fascinating and read it many times to really understand your reason for writing it. That was when I started getting similar dreams as you had detailed. At first, I thought it was because I was thinking about it and you that the dreams were coming to me. But later, I could sense that it was like thoughts were being implanted in my mind.

I say that it was being implanted because these were not coming to me in the normal way of seeing dreams. When I am awake, this comes to my mind, and when I see it during my sleep, it will still be very clear when I wake up. I don't forget any point in the dream.

It was invariably about a person spinning at top speed and an apparition with no form appearing next to him. It would end with the shapeless form pushing the spinner down on the floor.

I did not care much about all this. But after reaching our desert camp that day, I had to believe that there was really some connection. The spinner whom I saw in my dream almost resembled Ahmed Mansour. But instead of Mansour, you were the person who fell from the floor. I could see the spinning shape pushing you down. It was as though it did not like your interference with Mansour.

I have no explanation for all these things which happened to me, but I fear something bad may happen if you go again to that place in the desert.

Do you remember the way I slid down from the camel that day? I became afraid that time that I would fall down. But more than that, I got a jolt when I saw in front of me the same apparition I had seen in my dreams. It was there in front of the camel, and it was as though it wanted to stop me from being there. Luckily, I did not fall down. But after that, see what had happened to you when you tried to reach out to Mansour.

I did not want to talk to you in detail in the presence of Mother since I did not want Mother to know about all these. She would get upset very fast.

But I wanted to caution you.

Two weeks back, I had a recurrence of the dream sequence for three days. This time it was you going around the same desert to meet Mansour. I knew that the same unknown force was implanting these images in my mind. Maybe it wanted me to warn you. But I don't want to complicate things for you.

Dad, take care of yourself! And keep me informed of what you are up to so that I too can convey to you if I see something strange.

I once again read your article. By the sense of conviction with which you had written it, I am quite sure you would follow this till you find the answers. One way that is better than being in the dark. So if at any time you feel the necessity of an assistant in this search, call me!'

That was definitely strange. But it made me more resolute. I had to see this through the end.

Since Kav had got involved in this, I decided to inform her of what happened during my return visit to the desert to meet Ahmed Mansour. At least that would reassure her and make her less nervous.

I should let her know how this mystery was mired with mysticism!

CHAPTER 8

Meeting With Mansour, The Mystic

I had to clearly write to my daughter, explaining all the things that had happened to me. Now that she knew half of the facts, it would be better that she knew the complete events. At least there would be one person for me to confide in.

I went over the events of the last fortnight.

I had resolved to find out the truth behind these occurrences from Ahmed Mansour. He seemed to be the only person who knew about the true facts. Therefore, finding him was the first thing to do.

I went to Dubai and contacted Yousef, the driver of the Hummer who had taken us to the desert before. I booked the Hummer for myself and told Yousef to take no other passengers. For him, it was a strange request.

On the drive to the desert, Yousef was very eloquent in explaining his life in the desert—twelve long years of friendship with the sands of the desert. He had vast experience in driving over the dunes and had seen many accidents during his time. He was of the opinion that over a period of time, the desert had been filled with the lost souls of all those victims of accidents and of rage and vengeance from the olden days of war and anarchy in the desert.

He had many tales of how he had helped a number of tourists, including film personalities from India.

When I told him about my intention of meeting Ahmed Mansour, he was truly surprised. But I lied to him, saying that I wanted to learn more about the tanoura dance since I was writing a book on several ancient dance forms. This doused his curiosity.

We reached the camp. Yousef knew the manager of the camp, and we directly went to meet him in his office.

Enquiries regarding the whereabouts of Mansour revealed that he had met with an accident during one of his performances and was hospitalized in Jebel Ali. The accident was not very serious, but he broke his left arm and had to stay in the hospital for ten days to recover. He had fallen off the dance floor and landed on the ground with his left arm under his body. This impact was enough to break his arm.

I took a long breath. It seemed that finally that seventh guy succeeded in pushing Mansour out.

After taking note of the address of the hospital, we left the camp. Since I did not want Yousef to be with me when I talked to Mansour, I decided to go to the hospital the next day. So I got myself dropped off at ZiQoo Hotel at Discovery Garden.

The hospital was not so far away from the hotel. I could locate Mansour very easily. He was relaxing on his hospital bed and was in a separate room. This was good for me since what I was about to talk to him was not for the ears of any others around.

Mansour was not very surprised to see me. He greeted me with a firm hello, and I introduced myself. I told him the reason of my being there, and he listened to me very intently. After hearing my side of the story, he began.

What I heard from him promised a deeper mystery to be followed. And I knew I had a long way to travel.

Mansour was from a place called Konya in Turkey. Their family originally hailed from Egypt, but due to religious reasons, they had migrated to Turkey more than a century back. His grandfather was still in his ancestral home in Konya along with his grandmother. His own parents had shifted from Konya to Ankara and lived there.

Mansour's parents were in Dubai in the centre of the desert, while he was being conceived and that was the basic cause of all his troubles.

They were from a specific religious sect called Sufi, which was a part of Islam. His father had left Konya in the late sixties, looking for better pastures, and landed in Dubai. He got married to the daughter of one of the sheikhs of the desert and settled there.

Mansour had learned the tanoura dance from his father when he was a child. His father was an expert in tanoura and used to perform for visitors who frequented Dubai from many places.

But they never had a peaceful life in the desert. Mansour remembered that, as a child, he used to be afraid of people attacking them in the dead of the night. The howling wind would always bring some bad things to them. When he was about eight years old, the whole family had a major accident in which their house got burned down. Luckily, all of them escaped with only minor injuries. But with that, his father decided to leave Dubai and go back to Konya.

In Konya, Mansour stayed with his grandparents. From them, he learned that his father had gone out of Konya in spite of his grandfather warning him several times. Now they were happy that all of them were reunited with them.

Mansour loved his grandparents so much that he stayed back in Konya when his parents moved to Ankara. He studied in the local school and continued to practise tanoura, but for the religious rites of the Sufis.

Then he had this urge to go to Dubai to revisit the place of his childhood and see what new things had happened over there. The developments happening in Dubai were well known everywhere, and Dubai held a lot of promises to the youngsters.

His parents and grandparents agreed to his trip to Dubai, seeking some job over there. His grandfather had specifically told him not to go to the desert where he was conceived. Even though he asked him for reasons, he did not get any answers from his grandfather.

Once he was in Dubai, his curiosity overcame his wariness, and he started working for the dance troop performing in the camp where I had met him.

And his troubles started within a few weeks of being there.

The same apparition whom I had seen was always troubling him. He knew that this thing, whatever it was, was trying to stop him from doing the dance or was trying to somehow harm him. But when he was fully engrossed in the dance, he could never be harmed since his mind would only be thinking of divine things. He would be full of thoughts of God, and no outside force could penetrate his mind. He was that strong mentally.

But whenever his mind wavered while performing tanoura, he would feel that thoughts were being implanted in his mind, and that was how he could understand my thoughts when I went to see his performance that day. He knew that somehow both of us had the same thought waves. The frequencies matched, and we could see the same things connected with the apparition.

It was at such a time when he had momentarily lost his concentration that the seventh guy, as I had mentioned, pushed him off the floor.

Mansour was happy that I came back to meet him. This gave him an opportunity to share his feelings about the tanoura and the desert. And that day, together we decided to find the truth about this.

Mansour suggested that the first person we should meet was his grandfather since he knew a lot about the mysticism in their religion. If we started from there, we should be able to understand the reasons and the probable method to come out of this trouble.

Mansour should be fit to travel within three weeks as per his doctor's instructions. After moving into the hospital, he never had any problems with his desert foe. So he had planned to spend the three weeks in the hospital itself till he could move around.

We decided that by the end of the month, we would travel to Konya to meet his grandfather.

I asked Mansour to relax and assured him that I would organize flight tickets for both of us. There was no need to immediately inform his people in Konya about his return. Instead he could let them know of his travel plans closer to the date of travel.

We exchanged our mobile numbers so that we could keep in touch with each other, and I made him promise that he would call me for anything that he might require. Since I keep driving to Jebel Ali for my weekly meetings at the head office, it was easy for me to help him any time.

That was how we met and became good friends—friends with similar thought frequencies.

I was looking forward to the trip to Konya and wondered what strange things it held for us. It was an exciting thought, but all the same, the danger both of us had been encountering due to our thoughts kept me feeling apprehensive.

CHAPTER 9

The Turkish Connection

I finished writing to my daughter. I put the letter in an envelope and sealed it. I would send it the same way she had sent me her letter—by ordinary post. She was right in saying that an ordinary post would be less conspicuous than any other type of mails. We did not want any other person to get involved in this.

I had promised her to keep her informed about our trip to Konya. I had also cautioned her not to think too much of this so that she can avoid unnecessary thoughts being implanted in her mind as it was happening recently.

I got the letter posted and let the monkey mail do its job.

Now that I knew Mansour well, I was very confident that we could together unravel the mystery during our trip to Konya and the proposed meeting with his grandfather.

I started planning for the trip ahead. I had to understand the best way of reaching our destination. I contacted our travel agent.

Turkish Airlines had daily flights to Istanbul from Dubai and had the flights from there to Konya. It would take about five hours to Istanbul, and a waiting time of about two hours before we catch the flight to Konya, which was a short flight of seventy-five minutes only. I got the flight tickets booked for both of us tentatively.

Time went by very fast. I kept myself busy with my official work. In between, whenever I had meetings in the Jebel Ali office, I would drop in at the hospital to chat with Mansour. These informal chats brought us closer to each other.

I learned a lot about their family in Konya. The description of the place, his house, and his family made me look forward to the trip so much. I was almost counting the days until our travel.

Normally, for Indian passport holders, most countries require them to obtain a visa in advance. Since I had a valid USA visa on my passport, I could get a Turkish visa on arrival, so there was no need to apply for a visa in advance. This was a big relief.

It was June, and the summer was peaking in the Gulf states. Towards the end of the month, Mansour got discharged from the hospital and was certified fit for travel by the doctor.

Immediately I got our tickets confirmed through the travel agent and got them issued. I contacted Mansour on the phone and explained to him our travel plans. He was very happy to travel with me and assured me that he would meet me at the airport.

It was a morning flight, and we met at Dubai Airport and checked in together at Terminal 1. While waiting at the gate for the boarding announcement, we started to talk more about the incidents of the past few weeks.

'The apparition which I had seen was almost certainly trying to be with you, Mansour. I had a feeling that whatever it was, it did not want me to interfere in its dealings with you. Maybe this has something to do with your childhood spent in the desert.'

'That's right, San. These deserts are filled with the souls of the people who had died gruesomely during the fights and bloody wars of the past. Through the centuries, the desert clans had been fighting with one another. It was only recently that Sheikh Zayed bin Sultan Al Nahyan brought the people together, and peace was returned to these parts.'

'So it could be one of those lost souls seeking vengeance. Is it vengeance on your father or you? You were too small when you left this place to have antagonized any souls or, for that matter, any person alive. So it must have something to do with the past. Mansour, I think that by spinning, you tend to become massless or reach the verge which demarcates matter from antimatter or the live world from the world after life. Maybe your spinning at a high speed takes you towards the outer limit of masslessness, and that could be the reason for the antimatter or the soul to reach out to you from the other side.'

'San, you are talking about very complicated things, which are at present flying over my head. I think our meeting with my grandfather can bring more lucidity to these thoughts of yours. Till that time, let us enjoy this flight and the beauty of Dubai Airport with its endless rows of duty-free shops.'

I had to agree with Mansour since I did not want to put him under undue pressure. Better to have with me a person of sound mind rather than a confused one.

Since I was going to Konya for the first time, I thought it was better to learn about this place than discuss matters which are beyond our normal comprehension.

The flight was very enjoyable as usual, being on a Boeing 777-300 with its entire splendour even for the economic-class passengers. Good food, nice selection of movies, and comfortable wide seats with enough leg space made the travel easy. I could watch an Indian movie, which brought memories of my hometown flooding my mind.

Mansour spent his time reading some book in Turkish which, he later told me, was regarding Jalaluddin Rumi, the founder of Sufism. This was something I too had to learn later while making my research into the paranormal activities taking place around me these days.

We landed at Kemal Ataturk Airport in Istanbul and waited for our connecting flight to Konya. The airport was very nice, with all modern amenities available in the lounges. Even though it was not as big as Dubai's, it was constructed and decorated in a good way and had a pleasant ambience.

The domestic flight from Istanbul to Konya took only about an hour. It was almost like taking off and landing in a hurry. So finally we had reached our destination—Mansour's hometown of Konya.

I was wondering what mysteries awaited me in this mystic place. From the description of Konya I heard from Mansour, I knew it is a beautiful, peaceful city with very loving inhabitants. It has a very old culture dating back centuries. Most of the old families have known one another since the population was not very high.

We took a cab from the airport and started off on the short trip to Mansour's house. The sun was almost on its retiring stage and the yellowish brown skyline was a welcome sight.

The first stretch of road was almost through deserted neighbourhood. There were not many buildings on the two sides of the road. After about ten minutes, the buildings started appearing.

We drove past many buildings, which had the old architecture, making them elegant. The mixing of the new with the old seems to be a Turkish trait.

The roads were not so wide. Maybe after seeing the broad highways of Oman and Dubai, I felt that these roads were narrow. In fact, the lanes were marked well, and most of the time, we were on a four-lane track divided by a median of not-so-tall trees.

By the time we reached Mansour's house, the street lights were on announcing the arrival of the night.

Mansour paid off the taxi, and we entered his house, carrying our bags.

The sight of the old man with peaceful eyes and a face teeming with brightness indeed had a soothing effect on us, the weary travellers. I knew that this person, whom I guessed rightly as the grandfather of Mansour, would be able to render solace to our troubled minds and find answers to the umpteen questions we had framed in our hearts.

Mahmoud, Mansour's grandfather, was in his late seventies. He was of average build and looked very healthy.

Mansour's grandmother, a frail lady, also appeared by the side of the old man. She embraced Mansour and could not hide her happiness in seeing her grandchild.

They showed us our rooms and asked us to meet in the dining room after freshening up. The thought of a new cuisine made me hungry.

I had tasted Turkish food with my Turkish colleagues in Dubai. The Turkish restaurant in Sohar just next to where we were staying emanated such nice aromas during the evenings. Even though I did not eat meat or fish, the smell of grilled food was always a mouth-watering experience.

I took a quick bath and felt very much light. Now I was ready for a long night listening to Mahmoud.

Mansour came to my room and took me to the dining room.

There was a good spread of snacks. Even though I could not name all the items, I could distinguish samosa, cutlets, and falafel. I filled my stomach with a variety of vegetable-based items. Eggplant seemed to be a common ingredient in Turkish snacks.

All the snacks were very tasty. Mansour told me the names of these items, but the names did not stay in my mind since I was much too keen on devouring the tasty ones.

I thanked his grandmother for the nice welcome food. Then we got up to go towards the drawing room, where Mahmoud was waiting for us.

CHAPTER 10

Theory Behind Spinning

Mahmoud, even though in the seventies, was very strong in his mind. The sharpness of his thoughts could be sensed in his speech. He settled on to a large pillow behind him. We were sitting on the thick carpet. The smell of incense had filled the room. It rendered a pious atmosphere.

We were sipping the hot Turkish coffee offered to us. The special bond between Mansour and his grandfather was obvious. They respected and loved each other so much that the way they greeted each other gave me a sense of family love.

Mansour had briefed his grandfather on the motive of our trip to Konya.

Mahmoud started his narration, 'Sufism has its roots in this very place. Even though it existed in different forms, an organized method to follow the prescribed discipline was established in the twelfth century. It was a part of Islamism, but was being followed in a more mystical way.

'The Sufi whirling or Sufi spinning is a form of meditation. Normally, people meditate sitting or, in some cases, standing without any motion. It is said that certain sadhus of Hinduism sit for hours in the Himalayas without breathing. But in Sufism, meditation is observed by concentrating in spinning oneself.

'The spinning is a fixed way for keeping your hands, body, and legs all aligned with nature. The basic belief is that everything in the universe is spinning around a celestial body while also spinning on its own. You know that the planets are spinning on their own axis and at the same time moving around the sun. The theory of spinning is based on the movements of the planets in our solar system.

'Similarly, in Sufism the approach to godliness is based on spinning. But in my studies of spinning, I have been fortunate enough to find more dimensions to spinning than what has been taught during our religious upbringing. I will dwell on this theory later. First, let me make you aware of the inner meaning of the whirling which we practise.

'The particular way in which the *semazen*, one who practises sema or the whirling type of physical meditation, is dressed is based on the true meaning of the principle of Sufism. The camel-hair cap represents the tombstone for the ego. That means you have to shed your ego, which is the main reason for anger and hatred. His wide white skirt is the ego's shroud. In the beginning of the ritual, the dancers remove the black cloak. This way, by removing his outer shroud, he is being reborn into the truth within himself. The white garment with long sleeves shows the peaceful mind of the person.

'In the beginning of the dance, the performer will keep his arms crossed over his chest, representing the number one, which shows the unity in God and the oneness of the Almighty. While whirling, he keeps his arms open, with the right hand open to the sky and the left hand open to the earth. The right hand is ready to receive the beneficence of God, who is thought to be always above us. The left hand transfers the spiritual gifts from God to the earthly mortals who are watching the *sema*. Thus, he acts as a messenger or medium or, more scientifically, a transfer point between God and the earthlings.

'The semazen revolves from right to left around his heart to show the love with which he embraces the whole humanity.

The message of love and the penance he carries out for the good of mankind are being transmitted through the ritual.

'You can imagine how difficult it is to keep spinning at the same speed without a break. That is the skill the semazen acquires over years of training. Scientists say that any person who can spend more than 10,000 hours practising the same activity will become a master of that. That is why the parents start to send their children to learn different art forms from the time they are tiny tots of three or four years. This helps them to master their interest by the time they become twenty or so.'

I was happy to hear the same reasoning I had conveyed to Jai before about practising an art. Even though I had casually read about this, now it seemed to me that the author was authentic about it. Even this learned person who lived miles from that author had repeated the same words of wisdom.

Mahmoud continued his explanation, 'The semazens start their practice very early in their lives. They are attracted towards this form of religious penance by which you show your obeisance towards the Almighty. It is not possible for all believers to be able to practise sema and move towards God in unity. Therefore, those who are truly devoted do the penance for the sake of all in the community.

'Now you will understand why I told Mansour that a religious Sufi like him should not be doing a tanoura in the desert. That will definitely bring disaster. It is not God who will punish you, but you make even God helpless by moving towards the devils by this act. That is exactly what had happened to Mansour.'

Mahmoud stopped.

We were sitting with our mouths almost open, trying to digest each word being uttered by this grand old man. His wisdom poured through his words, and we did not want to miss even a single syllable from him.

From Mansour's expression, I could make out that he had not thought so much about the talent he had which he had misappropriated till now. He had made a big mistake for himself, and unknowingly, I too had become a part of it. This was a rather curious coincidence which I could not explain. But I put in my mind that I should check with Mahmoud about that specifically. It would definitely be interesting to know. This great man will have an answer to my query.

Mahmoud was looking at the coffee flask, but the flask was empty. As though by intuition, Nargis, Mansour's grandmother, walked in with a new flask of coffee. She poured it for us, and we eagerly sipped it as if to energize us to take the full impact of Mahmoud's words.

Mahmoud continued, 'Sometime in the twelfth or thirteenth century, Sufism spread to other Islamic Arab states. In Egypt, they accepted the rituals of spinning but soon commercialized the art form of the dance. Rather than practising it as a part of religious meditation, they were using it to entertain customers.

In Egypt, they call this tanoura, and you would have experienced in the Dubai desert the tanoura being performed by Mansour. This was combined with other entertainments like the belly dance.'

His voice hardened, and he looked at Mansour. 'How can you ever think of performing the tanoura along with the Egyptian belly dancers? I had pleaded with you not to go back to that desert. But in spite of my warning, you went, and now you are suffering for that. You are a Sufi, and you are not supposed to dance for entertainment. Why would you do that? There are a number of other people who might learn and dance whatever they want, be it tanoura or belly dance. You should never have ventured into this.'

Mansour kept his head bowed down. Without looking into the eyes of Mahmoud, he murmured that he was sorry for that and intended not to ever repeat this mistake.

Mahmoud seemed to have accepted Mansour's apology. 'Okay, okay, Mansour. Now listen carefully. The mixing of tanoura and Sufi whirling by a born Sufi is not acceptable to religious functionaries. The Almighty will never harm us. Like a child misbehaving and his mother always forgiving her child, the Almighty forgives us who are his children. But at times he will not be able to help you out when you are in the hands of the ultra-negative forces. That is what happens when you are in the desert which is full of bad blood from the centuries of uncivilized ways of living.

'It is believed that any place on earth can be filled with departed souls. The attitude of good people will remain positive and that of the bad will remain negative even after they die.

'What I could gather from years of meditation and research is that the souls remain in those areas where they were let out of their physical bodies and influence the humans being born in those areas. Anyway, more of it later.

'If you have to understand about the positivity and negativity of souls and how they behave, you should know more about the theory behind spinning. Sufism had formed the whirling ritual for a specific intention. In those days, they had inner eyes to find out more about life than us.

'When you are spinning with great concentration, you are moving into nothingness. The speed of the spinning and the concentration of your spirit on the Almighty tend to make you approach a state of bliss, which is close to the layer that separates the living souls and the souls of life after life. The soul remains in this world with a specific form attached to it, and when it is on the other side of the world, it will have no mass or shape.

'In the Sufi ritual, you are in deep concentration, and you are only thinking of the Almighty. In this trance state, no other force can affect you since it cannot pierce your mind when your mind is fully devoted to the Almighty, the centre of all that are spinning perpetually.

'But when you are performing the same ritual with the intention of entertaining others, your mind is not fully turned towards the central spirit. It wavers and gives an opportunity for other external forces to overcome your concentration and thus enter your mind. This happens without your knowledge. You might be thinking why it happened only to Mansour. There is a reason for that.

'Mansour is a natural Sufi, and his life is supposed to be dedicated to the religious spirit with which we are all involved. He had learned his spinning through years of immovable love towards our basic intention. Therefore, his concentration is impeccable.

'But the normal tanoura dancers are practising their dance only for the sake of entertainment and are not so much dedicated to concentrating on one point. So even though for the onlookers they dance well, in reality they do not achieve the ultimate state of religious spinning. Therefore, they are still in the material world when they spin, unlike Mansour. Now you know why the unseen forces do not affect them. They reach nowhere near the plane of the departed souls.

'But Mansour can and will reach during those dances in the desert a state of masslessness. There lies the difference, and that is why Mansour is affected.'

I had a concern coming up in my mind. I put it forward to Mahmoud. 'Sir, how did you get the intuition of Mansour getting affected in the desert in Dubai? Mansour told me that he had announced his intention to go to Dubai in search of a job and to make some money for a good living, but you knew that Mansour would get trapped in the desert. How is that possible? Mansour is also perplexed with this forewarning from you.'

I looked at Mansour, and he nodded his head to show his concurrence to my question.

Mahmoud looked at both of us. 'You had travelled a lot. Are you not feeling hungry?'

Both of us said in unity that we were not hungry but wanted to listen to more of his observations and experiences.

Mahmoud did not agree. 'But I am famished. And the aroma of Nargis's cooking is making me more so. We do require a break for dinner. Let us eat well, and then we can go into more details. The night is still very young, and we have enough time to complete the story before sunrise. Come, let us wash and attack the kitchen.'

Reluctantly, we got up. But soon the aroma engulfed us so much that our stomach started to crave for the appetizing Turkish food.

CHAPTER 11

The Evolution of the Soul

The dinner was fantastic—the original Turkish cuisine. It seemed obvious how they keep themselves healthy even at this age. Just as the aroma of food suggested, the hands of Nargis were superb while cooking. Even though I was basically a poor eater, I had not enjoyed eating like this in the near past.

I tried to learn more about the dishes being served. Since Mansour had told his grandmother that I was a vegetarian, she made special vegetable dishes.

There was plain pilaf, which is rice cooked with butter, fried eggplant, pepper, and tomato sauce. Dolma cooked in olive oil and *mucver* were also nice to eat. Later I learned from Mansour that dolma is a dish of vegetables like tomato and eggplant wrapped in vine leaves. Mucver is a mixture of grated potato, egg, onion, cheese, and flour roasted in the oven.

Cacik is made from diluted yogurt and minced cucumbers; it was served as side dish, and it tasted delicious.

The Turkish coffee is a must after dinner, so we indulged in sipping the energizer while leaning on the soft, fluffy pillows.

After helping his grandmother in cleaning the dishes, Mansour also joined us. Now we were ready to listen to his grandfather. The excitement started brewing along with the coffee.

Mahmoud coughed a bit and straightened himself on the mat. Then he started his wonderful saga of the souls, 'Have you ever thought of how our body gets the soul formed into it and where the soul vanishes to when we die? This is a question many would ask themselves but find no answer at all. Many scientists have made many experiments to find out what the soul is, but have failed to come up with a logical solution.

'There is an explanation for this, which could be unacceptable to many. But for me, it is perfectly reasonable, and I have had many experiences to make myself believe in what I am thinking and saying to you now.

'It is true that if I am not convinced, I will not be able to convince you or others. I am convinced, but I have never ventured out to convince others about what I think is correct because it does not change their lives. But for me, it is important since we are in a situation where it matters a lot to the people who are immediately close to us.

'As I said, the spinning takes us close to nothingness, and that position is something which can cause things that are alien to the normal souls. It is like being on the edge of a precipice where a slight change in the balance of power can shift your equilibrium, causing you to fall on either side.

'So I had to learn more of it, and I had to protect the people around me. My years of study in this natural phenomenon had good effects on my thinking, and it shaped my reasoning power as well as concentration.

'Now coming back to evolution of souls, I have to talk to you about the positive and negative energies around us. Everybody talks about these energies, and some get a feeling about the relevance of these energies when they stay at a particular place. But have you wondered from where these energies or our feeling of these energies have originated?

'As you might have read in the books these days, at the time of the Big Bang, matter and antimatter were created. But as time moved on, we could see only matter, and we are not able to see or understand what we call antimatter.

'My studies made me understand that antimatter is a thing that has no mass or shape. This is the cause of the latent energies around us, which we term as positive and negative energies. These energies are the basic components of the soul. A person's character is decided by the type of energy which enters his body when he is conceived. The entry of the soul is completed within the first three months of pregnancy, and that is the period when the woman has to be very careful with the embryo inside her womb.

'This is the time the positive and negative energies fight with each other to get the space inside the embryo, and finally the strongest will prevail. The strength of any energy will depend upon the area where the conception has taken place. If that area has more of negative energy, invariably the child will get a character closer to a villain, and if it has positive energy, he develops himself into a person of good nature.

'A place where a lot of villainous characters have perished through the years will have a very strong current of negative energy with all the departed bad souls around that place. So the place where the husband and wife reside and conceive their children is very important in the formation of their children's characters at a later stage. That will be the inherent nature of that child—the nature of the energy which entered him during that time.

'The soul, being massless and shapeless, cannot be seen by the ordinary eyes. But when you spin at a very high speed and you approach the outer limit of masslessness, you get the power to see them and feel them in your mind.'

Both of us were dumbfounded with what we were hearing. It was not really going into our minds. This was really over-our-brain stuff that we were listening to. But the speaker had so much conviction in what he was saying that we were automatically nodding our heads in unison as though we understood the whole concept of the evolution of souls.

Mahmoud stopped talking, and there was silence around us for some time. I broke the silence by quipping doubtfully, 'Sir, can you explain a little more clearly? I think this is a little bit complicated for our normal minds to comprehend.'

Mansour's grandfather sipped his coffee and said, 'No problem. I will try to explain with an example which will be easier to understand.' He shifted on his pillow to change the direction of his lean and continued, 'Let me tell you about Mansour since he and his problems are known to you. This will also make you understand the reasons for his problems.

'Mansour's father, Ali—that is, my eldest son—did not want to continue with the rituals we have been practising in our house. He had a different thinking, and I never stood against the wishes of any of my children. I had always allowed them to choose their own way to grow.

'Ali had travelled to many of the countries in the Middle East and finally found his place in the desert of Dubai. There he had found his lady-love, Mansour's mother, and married her. I had no issues even on his marriage. But once the wedding was over, I insisted that he return to Turkey or at least leave the desert and stay in the civilized part of Dubai. I had heard about the cruel desert of Dubai, where lawlessness had prevailed many years before and a lot of fights between Bedouin groups had taken place. The people in the desert were ferocious fighters, and they had to resort to fighting for their survival. As they say in English, it was the survival of the fittest.

'Now you can imagine the atmosphere in those deserts and what type of energy would have filled the nothingness there. The negative energies always prevailed over the positive energies just by sheer number and their fierce nature.

'Rather unfortunately, Mansour was conceived in this area where the latent energy was negative. His soul was being formed by strong negative energy, the force of which was so powerful that Lubina, Mansour's mother, had several bad things happening to her frequently. She was slipping and falling often and had little accidents in the kitchen. Her mind became too confused with it all, and she was afraid to do anything.

Ali at last sent word to me about his problems through some friends travelling back to Konya. I realized the thrust of negative energy and immediately requested him to return to Konya. Luckily for me, even though the village doctors told them not to travel before three months are over, Ali heeded my advice and returned to Konya. The travel at that stage was very bad for Lubina, but she felt the reversal of her bad health the moment she entered our house.

'Then onwards, Lubina was very happy, and finally Mansour was born here. Since she had travelled before the completion of three months, Mansour's soul was not fully developed yet, and the positive energy prevalent in this area prevailed over the negative which was already inside him. So Mansour grew up as a well-behaved child.

'Ali still did not understand his folly, and he insisted on going back to Dubai. He gave the excuse that since he had come back without any planning, he had left most of his belongings back in Dubai. So after about six months of Mansour being born, all three of them returned to Dubai. Lubina also wished to be with her parents.

'I had warned Ali that in case he finds any problem, he should immediately return. But it took him several years and many disasters before realizing his mistake. At last, the house getting burned down really made him think and return to Turkey. That is Mansour's background. Now you might have guessed why I was reluctant to allow him to go back to that desert.

'But Mansour was headstrong like his father. He was a good student and learned the Sufi whirling in the right way and could involve himself to the core of its essence. He was doing very well while he was here. Then the Dubai bug bit him, and one day he wanted to try his luck in that magical world. I cautioned him to stay away from the deserts. But I did not explain to him all these because I did not want him to get weighed down with such a big burden on the truth of his birth.

'He made two mistakes—going to the desert and then performing the holy dance for entertainment. Both were absolutely not good for him. The negative forces easily recognized his soul, which was a bit part of them but was changed almost fully. That bit part was more than sufficient for them to force themselves in again. But Mansour being too much engrossed in his spinning could not be overpowered by those souls. So they were always around him, trying to push him so as to make him lose his concentration, and thereby they could get a chance to break in.

'The apparition you saw next to Mansour, which you termed as the seventh guy, was one such spirit. You saw that it was trying to push Mansour, but Mansour was oblivious to what was happening. Yet at times when his mind was wavering, he could sense the presence of those apparitions, and when you appeared in front of him, Mansour could immediately relate the facts. You have a nature similar to his.'

Mahmoud stopped talking since I had raised my hand to interrupt him. 'Sir, in what way are Mansour and I similar? I can't find any similarity other than us seeing the same apparition.'

Turkish coffee seemed to be Mahmoud's weakness. He was having it in abundance. The coffee tasted very good, and each sip gave us an added impetus for knowing more about these mysterious happenings around us.

Mahmoud continued from where he had stopped, 'Your thinking was similar to that of Mansour. Mansour knew about the spinning and its divinity, but he was ignorant about the inner truth regarding the evolution of the soul and the swirling's proximity to the souls. He did not consider this till the time he experienced the effect of it in the desert.

'You had that dream because of many reasons, as you know, and you had the thirst to gain more information about this. Your quest for the truth behind this brought you to Mansour, who was the closest in having similar thought waves to yours.

'If you want to borrow the words of the elders, it was destiny which brought you two together. Destiny is nothing but the work of the positive and negative charges forming the base of one's character. They push you towards the end they want you to have. If the positivity is stronger than the negativity, you move towards glory. Otherwise, the end will be more of villainy.

'Mansour tried to warn you to stay away from him since he knew that you also saw the apparition. You had not practised any form of concentration of mind and, as such, were very vulnerable to the attack of the negative charges predominant in that area. What they could not achieve when Mansour was conceived, they were trying to manipulate at present since Mansour had played himself into their hands.

'They did not want you to interfere in their plans, and that was why with one push they sent you out of the place. Your mind was not as strong as Mansour's, and the questions regarding the meaning of your dream on spinning were confusing your mind. That was why, in a moment of uncertainty in your mind, when the Hummer was going downhill, the apparitions appeared in front of you. Both the negative and positive parts were there, pushing at each other, one trying to make the other stay away from you.'

Mahmoud was concluding his talk. 'I think I have given you enough to think about for the night. You should try to get some good sleep. Tomorrow Mansour will take you around Konya, and you will get first-hand knowledge of the culture of Konya and its Sufism. You may have more doubts about all these facts. We can again sit after dinner tomorrow to discuss more about this. Tomorrow it should not be me talking so much. I would like to know about your experiences and how you see these events which have touched your life so forcefully. You have to be strong—not just strong, but very strong—in your mind so that you do not succumb to the taunting of the negative antimatter.'

We said goodnight to one another and retired to our bedrooms.

CHAPTER 12

Halo of a Healer

I got up early in the morning. I thought I was quite early to wake up, but Mansour's grandparents were already awake and had started their routine. It was just like the routine you could find in our household back in India. All the elders would wake up so early in the morning. Only the youngsters would be reluctant to get up and would keep sleeping till the sun burned their backs.

The strong tea provided by Nargis was really an energizer. I totally relished the tea. I used to pride myself in that I make very good tea. But now I realized that I did not know how to make good tea.

A nice steam bath was followed by a very healthy Turkish breakfast. The Turkish word for *breakfast* is *kahvalti*, which means 'before coffee'. Mansour told me that *kahwa* is 'coffee', and *alti* means 'under'.

I had vegetable soup and *menemen*, which was prepared with tomatoes, green peppers, onion, olive oil, and eggs. Mansour was having spicy sausage along with lots of vegetables. The breakfast was so relishing that it made me look forward to lunch and dinner.

After breakfast, I went out walking with Mansour. I was very curious to know the history of this mystic city and its Sufism. Mansour was a good teacher himself. He had got the flair for talking from his grandfather. He could explain things in very plain English.

'San, we shall go to the Mevlana Museum. It is actually the tomb of Jalaluddin Rumi, the founding father of Sufism. This has been converted into a museum, and it gives the history of Rumi. The place is about half an hour's walk from my house. I hope you do not mind walking.'

I was more than happy to walk. The walk would give me a chance to stretch my legs well and also I could see and enjoy the neighbourhood. A leisurely walk would ensure that I learn about the city in a good way from Mansour.

We walked, and Mansour kept showing me things related to his childhood. On the way, he met many people who instantly recognized Mansour and greeted him by saying, 'Gunayuddin.' This was the only word in Turkish I knew, which I understood as 'good morning'.

All the persons we met seemed to be concerned about Mahmoud, and they were always asking about the health of the old man and of course about where Mansour had been all these days. To some, he explained about Dubai.

When I got a chance, I asked him, 'Mansour, your grandfather is a very well-known figure in this city. Every one we met had been enquiring about him. Is there something else that makes him special to them? It seems to be something more than the elderly figure of your grandfather which makes them so close to him.'

Mansour took a deep breath and then answered, 'You are right, San. My grandfather is popularly known as Mahmoud the Healer. With his great wisdom in the ancient ways of Sufism, he imparts a healing touch to the poor people of Konya. I never could understand how he could heal people suffering from psychological problems and, to a certain extent, physical incapability also. They come to see him, and mostly within an hour of talking with my grandfather, they become all right. Only in very special occasions had I seen him extending the counselling session to two or three sittings.

'Over the years, Mahmoud had created a halo of a healer around him. He could understand others so fast and console them so tenderly that they become pacified and mentally soothed. The people around here have so much faith in him.'

I tried to tease Mansour. 'Then, Mansour, why don't you stay back and learn the powers of healing from your grandfather? No need to go to Dubai to become rich. Here you can become rich very fast with the right kind of healing touch.'

'Not a chance, San,' Mansour immediately quipped. 'Grandfather never takes any remuneration for the healing work he does. He believes that this is not his talent but that it is the grace of God which cures the people of their illness. I don't think I can ever inherit the charm and elegance of my grandfather. This is something out of this world which emanates from him.'

'I fully agree with you, Mansour. From whatever little time I had spent with your grandfather, I have generated a deep respect for your grandfather's stature. It is really greatness which surrounds him. The aura itself is having a soothing effect on whoever happens to be near him.' I had to agree with Mansour since I too had felt the effect while talking to Mahmoud.

'San, let me tell you something about the great Jalaluddin Rumi, who was the founder of Sufism. Rumi was born in 1207 in a village in Afghanistan. His father, Bahaeddin Veled, was a noted preacher and was known in those days as the Sultan of Scholars. Rumi's family fled during the Mongols' invasion of Mecca, and then from there, they came to the Sultanate of Rum.

'Konya was the capital of the Sultanate of Rum, which was ruled by the Seljuk. Rumi was a brilliant student of Islamic theology and was supposed to have studied in Aleppo and Damascus in Syria before returning to Konya. Rumi was a great poet, and his writings has found a place of high stature in English literature as well. He made Sufism the art of love. He wanted love to be the only credential required to becoming a part of Sufism. Tolerance and love were the central motives of the Mevlana's teachings. *Mevlana* means the 'guide' or 'master', which he was to everybody. That was why people started calling him the Mevlana very fondly.

'His famous words, which shows his heart for love, are repeated everywhere.

> '"Come, whoever you may be,
> Even if you may be
> An infidel, a pagan, or a fire-worshipper, come
> Ours is not a brotherhood of despair,
> Even if you have broken
> Your vows of repentance a hundred times, come."'

Mansour stopped. I thought he was thinking of his childhood while he was repeating the words of Rumi, the great Sufi.

I looked at Mansour, expecting him to continue, but Mansour was pointing his finger a little far away, nudging me to look where he was pointing.

I looked ahead and was taken aback by the view of the top of the turquoise tower. That was a magnificent scene I perceived.

The tower rose from the background of old buildings. The colour of the tower was exquisite. The buildings around the tower had been left as it is to give the mausoleum an ancient look. That was the tomb of the great poet Rumi.

Mansour held me close to him by the shoulder. 'San, when I see this, I remember the culture of love which has been given to us by this master of scholars. I had learned a lot through my grandfather about this man and his teachings. But somehow I became stupid in leaving this place when the dreams of Dubai took control of me.'

I comforted him. 'That is also an experience, Mansour. You always learn from what you do, especially from travelling. You must have learned a lot during your days in Dubai and more so in those days in the desert. These cannot be compared to any tuition from a teacher. You have to get a mix of all these experiences. They will help you a lot in your future and allow you to shape the life you want to have. So I would say that it was very clever of you to have spent time in Dubai. Now you will appreciate the things you have in your village more than you had done before.'

We moved forward. I was impatient to see the mausoleum and to learn more about this Rumi. I had not seen any portrait of Rumi and so could not form an image of him in my mind. I asked Mansour about Rumi and what he looked like.

Mansour asked me to be patient till we reached our destination, where I could get a first-hand view of the poet. Several paintings were there in the museum. He also mentioned that he did not want to kill the surprise by talking about the appearance of Rumi in advance. I started wondering what he meant by this surprise. Anyway, it was only a few minutes more to reach the place, and then I could come to my own conclusions.

As we neared the museum, the road seemed to be brimming with people. There were tourists who were going there to understand the culture of this ancient place and also local people thronged this place for worship. The tomb was a place of holiness for them.

We entered the museum after removing our shoes and leaving them by the side of the entrance.

Mansour explained to me the meaning of the inscription on the silver door, 'Those who enter here incomplete will come out perfect.'

We paid our obeisance at the tomb of the Mevlana. By the side of the tomb of Mevlana, there was another tomb, which had the remains of his son, Sultan Veled. The tomb of Mevlana's father was on another side of the room. The three generations of great men lay there, oblivious to the great respect which had been generated by their efforts during their days.

Mansour was in deep meditation for about ten minutes. I looked around, standing next to Mansour. For me, meditation does not come easily. The moment I close my eyes, my mind would start to wander around many things, past and future. I knew concentration was an art and that it should be practised. I made a mental note that I should also try to learn meditation. It was self-will.

Then Mansour took me to another room where there were many writings from the Holy Koran. All these were manuscripts dating back to the time of the Mevlana. Whoever had written these, the handwriting was really beautiful.

That was when Mansour pointed to a portrait at the far corner of the room. I looked at it, and a low cry escaped my lips. I thought I was looking at Mahmoud, Mansour's grandfather. They had so much resemblance. Now I could understand why the locals revered Mahmoud so much. It was not just the healing touch that he had but also the fact that he was directly connected to the great Mevlana himself.

Mansour was watching my expressions. Finally, he said, 'San, you got a real surprise, right? I wanted you to understand it directly rather than through me. The local people think that my grandfather is the reincarnation of the Mevlana.'

I was stuttering, 'Really . . . that was a surprise, Mansour. It is not only the facial resemblance alone. There is an aura which both of them share. I had never believed in reincarnation even though I had read many articles on the same. But with the recent events that had happened in our lives which got our lives intertwined, I could believe anything. Your grandfather and the Mevlana are almost the same, I should say. So much greatness in both of them, and their eyes impart a peaceful ambience to those who behold them.'

We went around the museum and saw every bit of it. I did not want to miss any part lest it may hold something strange and mystical shedding light on these old Sufis' ways of living.

The teachings of the great Mevlana were written in some places. Examples of the art of calligraphy were aplenty in the museum. Mansour translated many of the writings to me.

What struck me most was the following words of the Mevlana: 'Either be seen as you are or be as you are seen.' These words mean a lot. One has to be plain and true to oneself.

By the time we came out of the museum, we had started to feel hungry. I checked the time and saw that it was past noon. No wonder my stomach craved for Nargis's cuisine.

We walked back to the house. Mansour took me through another route so that I could see more of Konya. He kept talking a lot about the city and his childhood. My mind was busy with the thought of meeting the present-day Mevlana, our guide.

Chapter 13

Mahmoud and the Mevlana

No need to say that lunch was fantastic. I thought I was falling in love with this lovely Turkish cuisine. Maybe it was the magic touch of Nargis which makes this food so tasty and relishing.

We had our stomachs full. The main dishes were non-vegetarian, but there were a lot of vegetarian food for my palate. This time, I had *mercimek*, which was lentil soup, and *patlicanli pilav*, which was rice with eggplant. I had become fond of cacik, so I relished it. No need to mention the salads that accompanied every meal.

The dessert was a good spread of different sweet dishes and ice cream. I tried baklava and *kadaif*.

To top everything off, the coffee came with its aroma filling the air.

During lunch, conversation was very little, mainly connected to the food.

Later, we sat in the porch and enjoyed the breeze. It was a sunny day, but the breeze kept the heat away. I slowly closed my eyes and started to fall asleep.

My mind was full of images of the Mevlana and Mahmoud. Such resemblance. I could not wait to talk to him in the evening to understand the reasons for such likeness. Mahmoud was not in the house. He had gone out to meet some people and would return only in the evening.

I remembered Mansour telling me that many people would visit Mahmoud for getting his healing touch and sometimes take him away to their houses to meet the elderly citizens who were not healthy enough to come to him. Today was one of those days; Mahmoud had gone out to give solace to some ailing soul in the town.

This person was a mystery. He was such a loving and lovable figure. His appearance itself gave so much peace to the mind. No wonder people thought him to be the reincarnation of the Mevlana. He had healing powers, which would have been bestowed upon him by the Mevlana himself. With the events I had been going through, everything which had seemed impossible became possible.

With my mind full of the Mevlana and Mahmoud, I slipped into a deep slumber.

It was five in the evening when Nargis woke me up with a cup of steaming tea. That tea brought me back to my full senses. I had slept well. Mansour was sitting on the opposite chair and smiled at me. 'You had quite a good sleep.'

'Yes, Mansour. My mind was wandering around the Mevlana and Mahmoud. I cannot wait to sit with Mahmoud and see the rest of the leaves from his book of knowledge. The immediate and most important query in front me is why we two were connected. The two of us have nothing in common. But we got in touch with each other as though we had been friends for many years. How did our thought frequencies become the same in our case?'

'This is something only Mahmoud can answer, San. From what Grandfather had told us yesterday, I had a feeling that your weekly travel along that desert must have something to do with this. You were travelling very close to our camp, and your mind was in turmoil after you had seen the effects of spinning in your dream. Your dreams would have been caused by the triple effect of the things you had been thinking about—*Inception*, noetic science, and Hadron Collider. You had started to create your theory of spinning into oblivion, which was an actual fact in our lives in Sufism.'

I replied, 'That could be a possible explanation. This could have twisted my own thought frequency to be resonant with your thought frequency. Actually, it didn't need to be yours, but anyone who was executing the spinning with a concentration similar to yours could have matched my thought frequency, right?'

Mansour became more animated. 'Yes, that's it, San. I am blessed that it was such a nice person like you who had thoughts similar to mine. I am very happy now that we could travel together to find answers to common events questioning our intelligence.'

I pushed further. 'The negative energy which was trying to push itself into you must have easily found me to be the one coming to your rescue. Being a wandering soul would make it much stronger than us normal human beings. It knew that if I started to converse with you, you would realize your own folly in coming to Dubai and get away from them all. So it made a strong move to push me down from the dance floor.'

Mansour had his reasoning as well. 'If you had gone back to India, we would have never met again. But it was lucky for me that you were in Oman and were frequently coming to Dubai the same way. Thanks, San, for your perseverance to find an answer to your side of the mystery, which made me realize my mistakes. Even though we had met only once, you made it a point to trace me to the hospital. That helped us in beating that negative soul.'

I was not that comfortable as yet. 'We cannot say that we beat it as yet, Mansour. Maybe it can come back to me when I travel again on that road. My routine weekly trips to my head office will continue. Now that it cannot find you, it will try to reach you through me. This is something we have to stop. The how can be answered only if we know the why. The only way is to wait for the great Mevlana to come back.'

Mansour agreed with my point of view. Even if Mahmoud came now, he would require some time to relax before he could start to answer our questions. I was very eager to see Mahmoud now that I knew there was a strong relation between the Mevlana and Mahmoud.

We decided to take a walk. The streets were crowded since people had started to loaf around as they spent their evenings. I was very much impressed by the ancient look of the streets and the closeness most people had with one another. The compact-village cordiality was evident everywhere. Like what had happened in the morning, Mansour had to quench the curiosity of the persons he met about the stranger with him.

Mansour chided me, saying that overnight I had become a celebrity in their village. Any new person for that matter will rouse the inquisitiveness of anyone. That is a universal rule.

After spending about an hour around the streets, we returned to the house. By that time, Mahmoud had also reached home and was relaxing in his room.

I took a bath and became as fresh as ever. I was ready for the next round of conversation on paranormal activity, and I was very much looking forward to again meeting Mahmoud, the present-day Mevlana.

We were seated in the living room. I felt very comfortable relaxing on the mat and cushions on the floor. Soon Mahmoud joined us with a great, warm smile. His face was effusive with love and confidence at the same time.

Mahmoud looked at me while getting seated across us. 'So, young men, what did you find out by roaming the streets?'

I was ready with my question. 'Sir, how is that you resemble the great Mevlana so much? It is not only your deeds but your face and physique as well which are so much like the Mevlana's. People are looking at you as though you are the reincarnation of the Mevlana.'

Mahmoud replied, 'So you had been to the mausoleum. It is just a resemblance. Nothing more than that, my son! However, there is a chance that the positive energy from the soul of the Mevlana could have influenced me during my birth. This is the place where the Mevlana finally left this world. So definitely, as my theory goes, his soul should have been moving around in this area.

'Normally, the positive energy tries to fit into a mind and body of a new life which it feels would be of a similar creation of nature. The negative energy always tries to push into wherever it feels convenient. But positive energies are not like that.

'Just imagine yourself inside a deep well. As you go down deeper, the content of oxygen will be less, and other lethal gases could become more. These gases will influence your organic system so much that even when you are full of it, it will keep getting inside your system till you die of asphyxiation. Negative energies are similar to these gases.

'But imagine yourself inside an oxygen parlour. Once you have enough of the oxygen you require, your mind takes you out of the parlour. It does not try to suffocate you with more and more of it. Your mind becomes strong, and you have very clear thinking. The positive energies are like oxygen. It fills your mind to the extent required and puts you in good spirits.

'The positive energy which enters you during the time of your conception will decide your character and, in some cases, your physique and looks. Maybe the Mevlana's soul had influenced my birth, and later I could mould myself to a certain extent the way the Mevlana had carried himself around. Maybe I was fortunate enough to be so close to the Mevlana in my thought frequencies.'

When Mahmoud stopped to sip his coffee, I chipped in, 'But, sir, most of the people around talk as though you are the reincarnation of the Mevlana. For all of them to get the same feeling, there is definitely something divine which has happened. I too get the same feeling.'

Mahmoud gave me his broad smile. 'Anyway, I am not the major topic in front of us. We have to analyze the problems which haunt you and Mansour. Don't think that you have escaped from the negative soul which is after Mansour. I understand that you will be always travelling on the same road between Sohar and Dubai and are bound to cross the desert area. This will give this usurper umpteen chances to influence you and thereby try to bring Mansour back to that area.

'As I had explained earlier, the negative energy never stops from its task of entering another soul. So this becomes a hazard for you. We have to fully eliminate this risk of similar things repeating. In your case, your mind is developed by the positive energies of the place where you were conceived and born. So where were you born?'

I was a little bewildered with what I heard. 'I was born in Seria, Borneo. Seria is now in the rich Sultanate of Brunei. My parents were in the state of Sarawak, at a place called Lutong, the next big city being Miri. I think, the nearest hospital was in Seria, which is about fifty-six kilometres from Lutong. All these places were part of Borneo, an island under Indonesia, which was known as East Indies islands. But during the early sixties, North Borneo was annexed by Malaysia and is now known as the states of Sarawak and Sabah, and Brunei became an independent country. We left the place in 1962 when the civil strife started, and the rest of my childhood was spent in my hometown in Kerala, the southernmost state in India.'

'That's the reason,' Mahmoud started when I stopped my narration of my birth. 'As you moved away from the place where you were conceived, over the years the influence of the positive energy which had engulfed you became reduced. But depending on the way you live and exercise your mind, the effects of the positive energy will remain in you, and in normal cases, you don't have any negative effects.

'But in your case, being away from your birthplace for such a long period has affected the composition of your soul. With your positive attitude and positive work pattern, you had no problems till the time your thought frequency started matching with that of Mansour, who was at that time being influenced by the negative energies in the desert. Your being inculcated with the phenomenon of spinning into nothingness or, as you yourself had termed it, spinning into oblivion opened up your mind to the vagaries of mystic Sufism. This made your thought frequency match with the nearest soul similar to yours, which was Mansour's.

'The positivity in your mind was weakening, which gave ample opportunity for the negative energy to try to push itself into you. Luckily, both of you escaped from the clutches of this unseen demon for the time being. But now we should think of how to eliminate all possibilities of this demon making a comeback so that both your lives can flow smooth.'

I was close to being terrified with what I was hearing from this grand old man. The effects of my enthusiasm for reading had brought me to this place and level. Now I had to get from Mahmoud the key to unlock this enigma. Definitely, this Mevlana should be able to help me come out of this unscathed. He and only he had the powers and the knowledge to provide me clues to the route for escaping this demon and stopping it from torturing my life in the future.

My thoughts wandered to Kav. She also may get influenced if I don't come out of this. As my mind was intertwined with that of Mansour, her mind was moving in tandem with my mind. So unless I come out of this, she also could be exposed to the villainy of the desert devil.

'It is time for our prayers. Excuse us, San. We will join you soon.' With this announcement, both Mahmoud and Mansour left the living room.

My mind kept wandering over the things Mahmoud had told us. Maybe I had to go back to the place of my birth. Could that be a solution? It would be like going to a recharging station. I could get my positive energies recharged and strengthen my mind by being in familiar surroundings for my soul to get reenergized. I would check with Mahmoud whether this could bring an answer to the problem facing us right now.

CHAPTER 14

Sarawak's Old Oil Well

Another day had dawned, and I was seated in the bedroom with my MacBook Pro.

Mansour had gone out with his grandfather for some specific work in the city. They would be back only by lunchtime. So I was left to myself to spend the morning time.

I had lot of things to do. Yesterday's discussions with Mahmoud had left a number of questions in front of me. I had to search in Google to find out details of Sarawak, the place where I was during my early childhood days.

Yesterday night I had posed several questions to Mahmoud. I had to find answers to these questions: Why did the thought frequencies of Mansour and myself match, causing us to come together? Why was this negative soul so strongly behind Mansour? Was it safe for me to be in Oman and Dubai now that Mansour would remain in Konya?

Mahmoud had answered these questions during his discussions with us. He could somewhat quench our curiosity on these aspects. But then I had further queries which had no answers as of yet.

How did my daughter come to be involved in this even though she was far away in India? How could I become stronger than this negative soul so that I don't have to be scared of it any more? Could a trip to my birthplace rejuvenate the positive energy of my soul?

About the connection of my daughter to this event, Mahmoud was clear that the mental similarity of my daughter with me was the basic cause of her being pulled into this affair. The reading of the related article and her continuous thinking about it in the same way as I had been doing triggered the resonance of our thought frequencies. Since she was far away in India, the Dubai desert cannot affect her any more. But it was important that I get totally out of this so that she can be entirely safe.

For the balance of the two problems, Mahmoud wanted to understand more about Sarawak and its history. He said that the history of Sarawak where I was conceived and born could shed more light into the ways of overcoming this negativity from the desert.

It was important to know the source and the cause before prescribing a remedy.

So here I was, searching the Internet to get more details of Sarawak. Even though I had spent the first six years of my life in this place and very often my parents would talk about it, I had never bothered to get into the history and geography of Sarawak. Now it had become of paramount importance for me.

Sarawak is in the north of Borneo and was an independent state till its accession with the Federation of Malaya to form Malaysia in September 1963. It has an old oil well dug by the Shell Oil Company in 1910.

During the seventeenth century, Sarawak was under Sultan Tengah before the Sultanate of Brunei took control. It had a lot of problems during the nineteenth century, and during this time, James Brooke arrived in Sarawak. He assisted the sultan of Brunei to restore order and peace in Sarawak, and as a reward, Brooke was made governor of Sarawak and effectively became the rajah of this area.

James Brooke founded the white rajah dynasty of Sarawak and was in control from 1841 till 1888 when the state was placed under British protection.

He expanded his kingdom and did very well in bringing up the state till the time he expired in 1868. Then his nephew Anthony Brooke took over and was succeeded in 1917 by his son Charles.

During the Brooke dynasty, Sarawak was expanded at the cost of Muslim warlords and the local tribes. They ruled the state for more than a hundred years with a policy of paternalism in order to protect the indigenous population against exploitation from foreigners. The local tribes of Ibans and Dayaks helped the Brooke rajahs in their just rule, which was established in this state.

During the Second World War, the Japanese occupied this territory, and in 1946 the British annexed it from the Japanese.

It was explicit that the area of Sarawak had undergone much turmoil in the past, and a lot of people with the intention of looting and killing others had roamed free in these terrains. Mahmoud would categorize them under the bad souls or providers of negative energy. However, the prominent figures, like James Brooke and his successors, had very noble intentions to govern the land in a just way and make the people live in peace and harmony. Thus, positive energy is also equally high in this land.

In the twentieth century, they struck oil in the state of Sarawak, and the Dutch established the Sarawak Oil Company under the Shell Group. This added to the wealth of the country, and Brunei, Malaysia, and Indonesia were looking to annex this rich state. In 1962 the major discussions and problems had started to brew, and finally during 1963, Sarawak was joined to Malaysia.

It was interesting to note that in 1910, Shell established the first oil well in Miri and that the first refinery started operations in 1914 in Miri. My father was working in this company during the fifties till the time we returned to India in 1962.

I had very faded memories of Lutong, where we had resided. But I did remember the stilted wooden houses and jungle in front of our house where the local Dayaks used to live.

I was fully absorbed in my studies about Sarawak in the Internet. The time went off very fast. I broke my concentration when I heard the familiar call from Mansour. So they had returned from their work. It was lunchtime already, and suddenly I was feeling famished. It was another lovely session of delicacies from Nargis, which I relished to the core.

As usual after coffee, we sat together and started our discussions.

Mahmoud asked me about my birthplace, and I related the facts which I had gathered in the morning from the Internet. He was amused to know that Sarawak had an oil well in the past. He was weighing the negative and positive aspects of the data on the history of Sarawak.

Mahmoud started to speak, 'San, my son, you have to be careful when you travel to Sarawak. The best way should be to get hold of any good friends over there. If they're from the local tribe, it would be great. They would be able to lead you to the correct places where you could get rejuvenated based on the early days of your parents in this area.

'From your explanation, I believe that you should be concentrating in the belt from Miri to Lutong and, from there, to Seria. You should visit these places, including the hospital where you were born. It is not possible to pinpoint where your parents were exactly at the time of your conception and the growth of the embryo during which time the most prominent soul in that area would have made the impact on you as an embryo.

'Since the positive energy of the soul is still within you, most probably, when you are in those areas, it would be able to recognize the source and interact automatically. So it is important that you travel and spend enough time for the part of the soul within you and the part of the soul outside you to get an opportunity to identify each other and get together.

'It is unlikely that during this time any negative soul would try to enter you just because the positive energy within you is a little weak at present.'

I had my doubts ready to be quenched. 'But, sir, in the case of Mansour, it did happen. All these events are the result of the negative energy trying to overcome our dear Mansour. Could the same thing happen to me as well?'

Mahmoud seemed to be choosing his words very patiently in order not to upset me perhaps. 'There is a big difference between you and Mansour. In the case of Mansour, he was going towards the source of negative energy, which was taking him away from the realm of his positive energy. So here the positivity got weakened whereas the negativity was at a high peak.

'But you are moving towards the source of your positive energy, which in all normal cases would recognize you very fast provided you are close to the source. I cannot define any limits on the distance since this will entirely depend on the present state of the source.

'Only in cases where there had been a push and shove between two strong souls at the time of your conception can the problem come up now. I cannot comment on what could have happened so many years back in a place so far away from us. Let us face facts as they come. But one should be prepared to take backup action, and that requires knowledge and a little a bit of clairvoyance.'

I was a bit shaken with this explanation from Mahmoud. I would be almost heading towards the unknown. I have to be an astrologer to plan for this trip.

'At least you can advise me on the precautions to be taken so that I do not run blindly into unexpected troubles. You know that I am fully dependent on you for this.'

Mahmoud raised his hand as though to pacify me. 'Don't worry, my son. You will be fully briefed on how to tackle this problem before you embark on this trip. But I will require some time to think and assimilate the facts about Sarawak. You can plan to return to Oman on the day after tomorrow. Tomorrow we will discuss in detail about your trip to Sarawak.

'Meanwhile, my suggestion is that you should attend one of the rituals of semazens in Konya. I want you to fully understand the system and how they concentrate to meditate while swirling. You should know our method of spinning into oblivion so that you can dwell upon your own theory.

'Even though you would not be able to fully practise the swirling, at least you will know how the Sufis are able to do this. Maybe you can try a bit of it. You had wanted to do it in Dubai desert.'

'I would be very grateful if Mansour could take me to one of the rituals. I very much wanted to witness one of these after learning so much about it from you and Mansour. I really want to understand how the great Mevlana could come up with such a novel and noble method of cleansing one's soul through spinning into oblivion.'

Now Mansour broke his silence. 'San, I am ready to take you. Let us go today evening to our holy place. I will explain to you what I know about this ritual, and you can talk with the people over there to understand more. There may not be many who can speak English, but I can always translate for you.'

We got up to leave Mahmoud to his afternoon siesta. We too got some relaxation before we venture out in the evening.

The more I knew about Jalaluddin Rumi, the more I moved towards Mahmoud or vice versa. The more I see of Mahmoud and listen to his teachings, the more I was convinced about the fact that he was really the reincarnation of the Mevlana.

I was sure that when I visited the semazens' place in the evening, I would be more enlightened on Rumi and Mahmoud.

I was looking forward to a night of peaceful learning, but it was not to be as peaceful as I thought it would be. I was not actually prepared for the events that were to unravel that night.

CHAPTER 15

The Rituals of Semazens

Mansour and I had been walking for almost an hour. It was I who had insisted on walking around the city to understand more about this beautiful area and its inhabitants. The more I saw the city, the more I was falling in love with it. It had a combination of the old and the new. I think this is true with most of the places in this great country of Turkey. They had preserved the ancient buildings and culture even when they were modernizing their cities.

The people were learned and wore modern attire. But still they stuck to their culture and never pushed the old traditions out of their minds. I recalled that I had seen the same blend of the new and the old in Istanbul when I had gone there on official work two years back. The fact that I was working for a Turkish company made me more attached to this country. When people say Turkey is beautiful, I would feel very happy as though it was my own country. India too has this traditional mix of new and old, especially if you travel in Delhi.

Now we were in front of the familiar mausoleum of the Mevlana. My mind wandered away to the painting I had seen inside this building of Jalaluddin Rumi. Mahmoud had grown a similar white beard almost pointing downwards. The beard was dense and resembled snow. Normally, Santa Claus was depicted with a similar beard. The pointed nose and the high cheekbones made the similarity between the two more than what it naturally could be.

Mahmoud's way of dressing was also in a similar fashion. Even though the Mevlana and Mahmoud had a gap of many centuries between their lifestyles, the ways both of them behaved and lived were admirably the same. To top it all off, Mahmoud wore a large cap much similar to the one shown worn by Rumi.

Maybe Mahmoud knew that he was the reincarnation of the Mevlana, and that compelled him to adopt the behaviour of the Mevlana. But the knowledge and the solace emanating from those piercing eyes could not be something like make-believe. Those traits were inborn and the confidence which oozed from him just embraced the listeners as well. As Mansour put it, he was yet to see a person leaving his grandfather's presence without getting relief from his worries. Mahmoud had the knack of consoling even the most distressed souls.

By the time we crossed to the mausoleum, my mind was made up on the fact that these two great souls were one and the same.

All of us were lucky that the positivity of the great Mevlana still lived through the body of Mahmoud. The Mevlana created Sufism for the good of ordinary people, and that continues to do the work it was meant to be doing in this grand old city of Konya. Tolerance, forgiveness, and enlightenment—these are the principles of the Mevlevi order, and it remains to be so, which shows its greatness.

Mansour shook me out of my reverie. We had reached the temple of the whirling dervishes. He was telling me about the ritual of the Mevlevis. Since the whirling of the Sufis is also known as the sema, those who perform this dance are known as the semazens.

Dervish means 'the doorway', and this ritual is to open the minds of the people to the gates of heavens or to the abode of the Almighty. During this ritual, each one who performs the whirling submits himself to the powers of God, and those who watch them intently performing also move themselves towards the gates of heavens. That is how the minds become peaceful with this ritual. It is true that if you really believe in something or someone, then that would bring you peace of mind. This helps you concentrate your mind on one particular thing and keeps the mind from wavering thoughts. The music itself is something which uplifts one's spirits. It is really enchanting and keeps you engrossed in its effects.

When we entered the hall where the ritual was being held, the semazens had begun their performance.

Mansour was explaining to me, 'The first part of the ceremony represents a spiritual journey. The seekers turn towards God and truth through love, thus transforming themselves to unite with God. The camel felt hat worn by the semazen represents the tomb of the ego, and the wide white skirt symbolizes the ego's shroud.'

I interrupted Mansour, 'Ego is the root of all evils. If one can shed his ego, he will become peaceful, and his love towards fellow beings will increase multifold. It is important for each one of us to think within ourselves so as to get rid of our big egos. I am fully with your semazens.'

Mansour continued, 'That is exactly what we have been taught during our classes for sema. I have tried my best to shed my ego. I feel that to a certain extent, I did succeed. But then these Dubai dreams plagued me so much, and I went in search of my fortunes without listening to my grandfather.

Coming back to the ritual, the semazens keep their arms crossed at the start of the dance. The person standing at the back represents Mevlana Rumi. They will first rotate themselves past Rumi to get his blessings. As they swirl, they open their hands with the right hand extended in an upward inclination with the palm open towards the sky, and the left hand is extended downwards with the palm opened towards the earth. This shows that they are receiving the blessings of the Almighty from the heavens above and are distributing the same to the people on the earth.'

He stopped talking so as to allow me to absorb the whole scene unfolding in front of me. Since Mahmoud already gave this explanation to me, I could grasp the underlying principle and see the ritual being enacted there. As the semazens kept whirling, they picked up speed, and then they kept spinning at a constant tempo. They were oblivious to what was happening around them. They were fully concentrating on their task of reaching God to get his blessings for the sake of the poor and downtrodden on earth.

I could feel the tense atmosphere in all the people gathered around the semazens in the hall, intently watching their swirling movements. They too seemed to be almost in a trance similar to the semazens. When you believe in something, you really get absorbed in it.

I wondered about my theory of spinning into oblivion. Was it possible that these men revolving at quite a good speed could reach a point of nothingness? Could it be that they could reach out to the other side of the oblivion, where the antimatter remains as massless positive and negative energies?

But from the brief discussion we had with Mahmoud, it seemed to be not possible that these semazens would reach out to that extent where they become a part of the oblivion. The convergence will take place if, as in the case of Mansour, a specific soul spins in the opposite direction to reach out to somebody it wanted to meet with. Otherwise, this hall would have been a chaotic arena of soul searchers.

Suddenly, I felt a nudge on my ribs. I turned to face Mansour. He was whispering, 'San, look towards the far corner where the ladies are standing. There is one girl who had been watching you for quite some time.'

I was surprised with what he said. I did not know anybody over here, and how could it be that a girl was watching me? I looked at the direction Mansour was talking about and saw that there was indeed a girl looking in our direction. All others were watching the dance, but here was this girl intently looking in our direction.

Mansour was trying to pull my leg. 'San, I think she has fallen in love with you—something like love at first sight. Otherwise, why she should be looking at you when others are around? She seemed to be not aware of others around her.'

'Mansour, at this age of mid fifties, I don't think any girl can fall in love with me. She must have spotted you, and you are the one she is targeting. Better be a sport and relent to her looks.'

'No, San. It is not me she is looking at. Her eyes are focused on you. Sometimes these Turkish girls can really get crazy. So be prepared for the worst once the sema ends.'

I looked at her again. She was a good-looking girl. Anybody would look twice at her. She could be the right partner for Mansour.

But then I had a feeling at the back of my mind that I had seen her somewhere before. But she was a Turkish girl, and there was no chance of me having seen one before. Still the doubt remained.

Mansour woke me from my thoughts. 'San, I have a feeling that I have seen this girl before. But I cannot recollect when and where.'

I took this opportunity. 'See, Mansour? I told you she had been looking at you. You could have dated her sometime back when you were here in Konya and forgotten all about it. A typical Casanova!'

'No, no, San. When I was here in Konya, I was always a pious 'house-to-school and school-to-house' boy. No chance of dating in this ancient city. I must have seen her somewhere else.'

By then the sema had come to the concluding steps. So I brought my mind back to the present scene of the semazens. They were taking a bow to mark the end of their swirling. Now the silent hall started to buzz with the people talking in low tones.

We were walking towards the exit door when a commotion behind us made us turn backwards. We saw that girl rushing from the other end towards us through the crowd. People seeing her mad rush made way for her to run. But she did not care whether she had space to move or not. She kept rushing forward. When she was almost in front of me, I moved a little sideward to give her enough room to pass by. But she had her right hand raised halfway and, while passing me, just struck her hand on my right chest. I fell backwards with the impact, and chaos followed.

I triggered an avalanche behind me by falling backwards on to Mansour, who was standing just behind me, and Mansour fell on to the others behind him. There was a lot of shouting and cries of pain and the thuds of chairs toppling.

I managed to get up, and then I pulled Mansour up. We did not want to get embroiled in the melee any further. So we stepped out of the door, squeezing ourselves between the surging spectators. Once outside in the open, we paused to regain our breath.

We looked around. But the cause of the whole problem was not to be seen anywhere. She had disappeared from that whole scene. Was she mad?

Mansour was the first to open his mouth. 'San, that crazy girl, what did she do to you?'

'She struck me on the chest. It was so unexpected I could not keep my balance. Then I fell backwards on top of you. What a mayhem she has created! I still wonder why she was watching us all through the ritual. Was it only to hit me like that?'

'San, I told you that these Turkish girls could be crazy, especially the "modern maids", as they claim. But this one intentionally hit you, for sure. Is there any other connection between the two of you? How are you now? How do you feel where she hit you? Are you okay?'

When Mansour mentioned it, I felt the pain on my chest where she had struck me. I put my palm on my chest to massage the pain off. When I moved my palm across my chest, a piece of paper came into my hand. I was surprised as to how this paper happened to be on my chest.

I looked at the paper. It was blank on the front side. I turned it. There was something written on it, and that side was sticky. That crazy girl must have stuck it on my chest when she hit me.

Mansour joined me to read the writing on the paper. It was in neat handwriting written all in capital letters.

The first line read, 'I L U,' and the second line read, '2 M C H.'

Reading this, Mansour started to laugh uncontrollably. 'I told you, San, that crazy girl is in love with you. For making you understand her love, she made all these riots back there. So sweet of her to have stuck her thoughts about you on your chest itself! She must have wanted to convey her heart's feelings directly into your heart.'

'Mansour, how could you say from this small piece of paper that she is in love?'

'It is very clear. The first line is for "I love you". The second line says "Too much". My god, how madly she must be in love to write like this. Normally, they will only say "I love you". In this case, she also emphasizes that it is too much.'

'Now, come on, Mansour. The second line does not read *much*. The *U* is missing. She must have meant something else.'

Arguing back and forth, we walked towards Mansour's house.

The peaceful night I was looking forward to ended up as the most chaotic night after all. I was not sure whether we would be able to sleep with this paper looming above our heads.

I was pretty sure that it was not a message of love. No girl would be crazy enough to create such a scene for her love. She could have turned to so many other means to give the letter to me without having to thump me down. She could have easily met me outside the sema hall and introduced herself. I did not think that a girl talking to a man was forbidden in this country even though it had a conservative culture.

The message was something else, and we had to think well to crack the meaning. Maybe it would be just some simple solution, which could come to us if we think properly. But Mansour was making me crazy by talking about love at first sight.

My nagging doubt that I had seen her before became stronger. I was almost sure that I had seen her, and that could be the reason for her to have given this note to me. So there was some other hidden meaning to these seemingly normal letters.

We had to crack the puzzle.

CHAPTER 16

Not a Long Way to Lutong

We, Mansour and me, were walking towards uptown. After a lot of brainstorming, Mansour had told me that Konya had both downtown and uptown, as they normally express the two sides of the city. Downtown was the old part of the city, and uptown was the newly developed area. So we finally decided to search uptown to search for the girl who made us forgo our sleep yesterday.

We had long arguments late into the night to get to the bottom of the note left on my chest by the crazy Turkish girl in the sema hall. Mansour did not agree in thinking anything else into it, saying that it was a love message. For him, it was just a short form for 'I love you too much'.

I could not convince him that nobody would leave a message like that without giving a clue to where to meet or how to continue the love. A girl in love could not be so stupid. So definitely, she would have meant something else so as to give us a clue to where she could be found.

But Mansour was adamant that Turkish girls are sometime crazy. They become more so when they fall in love, and that too when it is love at first sight. My argument that no girls would fall in love with an elderly person fell on deaf ears. He said that some girls love men with experience. But I did not relent to his view. I pressed on with my logic.

I had thought of the *L* to be for *live*. That means the *U* must be for a place in Konya. When I explained this to Mansour, he got at least a little bit convinced that the girl was pointing to where she lived.

That made us search for any area starting with a *U*. Finally, the idea of downtown and uptown struck Mansour, and we decided to go in search of the girl uptown.

With the first line somewhat cracked, the second line was half easy. The first two characters should be *to meet*. But the *CH* remained a mystery since we were thinking of the name of a place or a house. We thought of *CH* as *corner house*. As to which corner, it had become another puzzle!

Mansour, being away from Konya for quite some time, was not aware of the latest developments in the city. He knew the old establishments and houses very well. That was when we decided that rather than wasting our sleep, it would be prudent to go uptown and search for something akin to *CH*.

We had to walk for almost half an hour to reach the area which was known as uptown. Looking around for a corner house made us suddenly laugh at ourselves. Right in front of us, we saw a new coffee shop, and the name of the shop was Coffee House. That abruptly solved our mystery of *CH*. After all, that girl had given us a very simple puzzle, which would point only the relevant people in the right direction.

Smiling broadly and congratulating ourselves for cracking a cryptic clue, we walked into Coffee House. There were many people either enjoying their coffee or having breakfast. Our eyes scoured the whole shop in search of our mystery girl.

Finally, we found her sitting at a corner table, studying the menu card. She must have been waiting for us without ordering anything. To spend time till we reached the coffee shop, she was learning each and every item on the menu. When we reached near her table, she lifted her head and saw us. Her eyes brimmed with joy on seeing us.

She got up and extended her hand to welcome us. We shook her hand one by one and settled on the nearby chairs.

I started to talk first, 'My dear lady, you have to get some medicine for me to ease the pain on my chest where you hit me so hard yesterday. You could have been a little soft so that all that chaos would not have happened there.'

She grinned. 'What was I to do? At that time, I had no other way of sticking the note on you. I was not sure whether it was you whom I had to meet. But your face seemed familiar, and I had to take the chance. If you were the wrong person, I was pretty sure you would not have bothered to solve the meaning of the letters I had jotted down on the note. You would have thought of me as a crazy girl in love.'

If my face was familiar for her, then it was true that we had met her somewhere. I could not control my curiosity. 'Where have you met me before? I too had a feeling that I had seen you before. Even Mansour also told me the same thing.'

Mansour interrupted, 'Before all that explanation, can you tell us your name? That way, we can do away with the words *lady* and *girl*.'

'I am Damla,' she answered. 'I had seen both of you in the Dubai desert. I was one of the belly dancers who performed the day you came there and fell from the dance floor when you tried to meet your friend.'

Immediately, Mansour quipped, 'That's why I felt your was face familiar. You were the one who replaced the girl who was sick for a couple of days. I had seen you in the camp but could not quite place you well.'

I too was relieved to know where I had seen her. The familiarity came from watching the belly dancers perform. Since their item was before the tanoura dance, I was still in good shape then. We told her our names. Now we were curious to know why she had wanted to meet us.

Damla began her narration, 'I am from Konya and had stayed with my parents all through my childhood. After finishing my studies, I went to Dubai to work and had a reasonably good job in one of the hotels as a receptionist. I was also looking after the housekeeping during that time.

'Once I had gone with some friends to the desert safari. The belly dancing held my fascination, and just for kicks, I started to learn belly dancing. My teacher used to take me to dance in one of the camps. Then something started to happen to me. I had crazy dreams, and the blurred forms of something not really having any shape started to haunt me. The more I wanted to get away from that place, the more I got entangled with that place. In spite of my inner mind telling me to get away, I was forcing myself to stay there.

'Then my teacher gave me an escape route by taking me to Mansour's camp as a stopgap arrangement for that girl who had fallen sick. I had never shared these crazy feelings with anybody else, and this is the first time I am talking to somebody about this.'

I had to intervene to quench my curiosity. 'Why was it that you chose us to relieve your burden on?'

'I am coming to that.' She was taking her time going into details. 'The day I was in Mansour's camp, it happened. I saw Mansour, and I always saw somebody moving along with him. It was similar to the thing in my dreams, that same shapeless entity!

'The next day, you came with your family. Normally, you must have been another of the numerous visitors who are attending the function in the camp. But when I saw you during my dance performance among the spectators, I could feel some connection between the two of us. Even now I am not able to tell what sort of connection I am feeling between the two of us.'

Mansour elbowed me. He turned to face me and winked at me. I knew he was going back to his theory of crazy love. But I was sure it was not that. It must be something to do with the energies around us.

Damla was continuing, 'When you entered the dance floor to go near Mansour, I saw the shapeless thing very clearly. I saw the thing pushing you out of the floor. I was greatly concerned for your life as well as that of Mansour. I got very much afraid also that three strangers are getting involved between themselves due to some crazy thing. I had thought of coming to you to discuss these things. But your fall and your sudden departure from that spot were something I had not counted on. So I missed the chance to talk to you.

'You might wonder why I did not get in touch with Mansour then. I had thought of doing so. But I restrained myself from contacting Mansour since I felt that if Mansour doesn't know about this shapeless thing haunting me, he would not understand me correctly. It may only lead to complications.

'I tried to continue to work there. But I could hardly concentrate in the dance. Then I heard that Mansour had a fall and had been taken to some hospital. That incident made me decide to quit that job in the desert, and I went back to my old hotel to continue my work as a receptionist.

'I found the work very disturbing. I was not behaving properly to the guests. I kept making mistakes. Then my boss, the hotel manager, asked me to proceed on leave so that I could regain my old smartness and rejoin them. I accepted his advice, so here I am back in Konya.'

'And that's when you saw us in the semazens' dance hall?' Mansour asked her.

She nodded in the affirmative. 'To get relief from my dreams and crazy brain, I started to attend the sema. It was giving me good peace of mind. Then you came, and again all hell broke loose.

'I was watching you from that far corner all through the dance. Towards the end of the dance, I felt as though somebody was pushing my mind to run. But I had to meet and talk to you so that I can get to the bottom of this mysterious feeling. So I wrote that little note. I did not want anybody else to get the note and read it. So I had to use some short forms. I knew that if you were the one whom I thought I had seen in Dubai, you would think well to crack the short form and find me. Otherwise, you will take me as a crazy Turkish girl showing her love to some stranger. I proved to be correct, no? You used your mind in the right way and found me here waiting for you.'

Mansour asked her, 'If we had not come today, what would you have done?'

'I had no other way to contact you. I would have come and waited for you every day till the time one of you met me here. That was the only chance I could take, and it indeed gave results.'

'That was pretty smart of you, Damla.' I wanted to compliment her for her honesty. 'But that doesn't explain why you made such a chaotic scene in the hall. You could have just walked up to us and pushed the note in my hand without others noticing you. But instead you created such a lot of fuss, and God only knows how many got injured in that melee yesterday.'

'That was not me who was doing all that. I told you that I felt as though somebody was pushing me. I tried to resist that unseen force, but could not do it for long. It pushed me towards you and made me run. There were so many people around me, and I did not care for anything in front of me. I must have knocked down some people, especially some of the girls who were near me. That force kept me running towards you, and luckily, I found some sense in me to stick the note on your chest. I am sorry that I could not control the impact and that I had to push you down with my thumping you like that. I kept running, and I stopped only when I reached my house.'

'What about your parents? Were they not with you?' Mansour asked about her family.

'My parents were in the house. I am the only child for them. They did not know about this problem, and I have not talked to them about it. Yesterday night, instead of going directly inside the house, which would have got them scared, I was sane enough to walk in our garden before entering the house. That way, I could keep all the problems away from my parents. I do not want them to get worried about me.'

Mansour looked at me. 'What should we do, San? Do you have any idea of solving this issue for Damla?'

I looked at Damla. 'See, we ourselves have similar problems.' I explained our story and how we had reached Konya. She was rather relieved to hear that Mansour was the grandson of Mahmoud. She had heard about Mahmoud a lot. But she never had an opportunity to meet the great man who resembled the Mevlana.

I was concluding our side of the mystery. 'Then the best thing for us to do is to meet Mahmoud and explain everything to him. He will definitely have some solutions for all three of us. Damla, you should come with us to Mansour's house. Let us talk to Mahmoud today itself since I will be leaving Konya tomorrow.'

Mansour was a little sceptical. 'We should go to Grandfather and discuss. But I wonder how some shapeless creature could connect all of us so well! There has to be some reason for the connection. My connection with San had been solved to a certain extent. Damla being pulled towards me could be explained by the fact that we have the same work environment. It must be those negative energies that the Dubai desert holds. But I don't see any route for the connection between Damla and San.'

Again Mansour had a naughty expression on his face. He looked at me and then at Damla. His eyes were asking me whether his old theory sounded good. I knew that if I allowed him to, he would again bring up the crazy love story, citing that as the connection between us.

'Let us forget that, Mansour. Now let us think forward. Where do you live, Damla? Let us go to your house. You should take permission from your parents before we go to Mansour's house. Otherwise, they would be worried about you.'

'No problem there, San.' Damla allayed my fears. 'They are not conservative Konyans. They had spent most of their lives outside Konya. So did I.'

Mansour and I were almost in one tone when we asked, 'Where else have you been?'

She replied slowly, increasing the suspense, 'Lutong. That is a place in Sarawak, which is a state in Malaysia. You may not be aware of it.'

We were awestruck and could not move or talk.

CHAPTER 17

More Theories Than Mysteries

We walked towards Mansour's house. But before that, we had ordered coffee for us and enjoyed the drink while sitting around the corner table. We wanted to get some time to discuss a little bit more on the connections before presenting them to Mahmoud.

Damla was also surprised when she learned that I too had spent my childhood in Lutong and was born in Seria, Brunei. That was a wonderful coincidence. As Mahmoud had explained to us before, parts of our souls could be made up of the energies—positive and negative—from the same soul source. This would explain the connection which Damla had felt when she saw me first.

But we had to understand more the uncontrollable pull–push effect she had felt when she was in the semazens' hall and the events at Dubai desert when she had met us there. For these, we had to necessarily go to Mahmoud. He would definitely have some logical answers to all our queries.

The coffee and the discussions made our minds clearer as to how we should present the whole thing in front of Mahmoud. Mansour called up his grandmother to inform her that there would be an additional guest for lunch.

We reached Mansour's house almost at the lunch hour. Mahmoud and Nargis welcomed us and directly took us to the dining room. The lunch was as usual fabulous and, at least for the time being, made us forget all our worries.

Then we settled in the drawing room on the comfortable carpet and pillows. Mahmoud came in and sat in front of us. The three of us were sitting as though we were in a classroom. Damla was a little bit overawed to be seeing the great Mevlana in person. Later she told me that Mahmoud was the exact replica of the Mevlana. Till then she had only heard tales of this great man. Now she became so happy to see him directly and to get an opportunity to interact with him.

We explained to Mahmoud what had happened at the semazens' hall the previous day and the discussions we had in the morning at Coffee House.

Mahmoud was very impressed with Damla when he learned about the note she had stuck on my chest.

'Damla daughter, you were thinking smartly. Even under duress, you could do things properly. That shows a clear mind and good usage of the brain. Can you tell me more about your parents and the life you had in Sarawak?'

'Thank you, Uncle.' Damla was seen to be a little nervous. 'My father was working in Shell's oil refinery in Miri, and we were staying in Lutong. As I could understand from San, they too were at the same place. Only difference is that they left the place in 1962, and we were there much longer after that. By the time my parents went to Sarawak, it was already a part of Malaysia. I was born in 1982 when we were in Lutong. Later on, when the oil wells got exhausted, Shell reduced their operations and cut down on the staff. Then most of the foreigners left Sarawak and went back to their native countries. We too came back during that time.'

Mahmoud's face brightened. I could guess that he was on to the answers very fast since my life and Damla's life in Sarawak almost matched except for the time period.

'That explains a lot of the things which had happened to you, Damla. As I had explained to these boys before—sorry, San, you are still a boy for me—your character is defined by the energies that enter you while you are being conceived and in the early stages of the development of the embryo. The souls of the people who had died in those areas impart the positive and negative energies to create the soul of the foetus. That is how people get different characters and develop different attitudes and talents.

'A place where lots of wars and cruel deeds had happened would naturally have negativity more than positivity and vice versa. Luckily for both of you, Sarawak, especially Lutong, seems to have kind souls rather than cruel souls. So both of you are blessed with good nature.

'But as you stay away from the place where you were born, you tend to lose the strength of the positivity, and for this, I was suggesting to San to get himself recharged by making a trip to his place of birth. Maybe, Damla, you should do this also. A visit will not harm you. On the other hand, it will strengthen you. How did you land up in Dubai?'

Damla narrated to Mahmoud what she had told us about her stint in Dubai. She had also left Sarawak when she was six years old, pretty similar to me.

When Damla had finished talking, Mahmoud took over the conversation. 'It seems Damla has lot of things in common with both of you boys. Till she was six years old, her life ran parallel to that of San. After that, she had come to Turkey and then pursued her ambitions in Dubai. This part compares with that of Mansour. No wonder she finally landed up with both of you. Now that the three of you are interlinked with the energies of your souls, you have to tackle it further so as to solve the issues together.

'Apparently, the negative soul which had trailed Mansour had caught hold of Damla when she was in the desert camps. Mansour, with his concentration attained from sema rituals, was always a step ahead of the negative energy. Since it could not directly enter Mansour, it had used Damla to pursue you. It was good for all of us that all three of you escaped from Dubai at the right time.

'Damla was working in Dubai, and that too in the desert camps. San used to travel along the desert camp road, and it was easy for the soul of a person like Damla, who was very much in harmony with the soul of San, to pull San towards her. That is how San got affected by the negative energy.'

'Now what should be our plan of action, sir?' I queried when Mahmoud stopped for a while to sip his Turkish coffee.

'San, as you know now, we do not have any mystery. But what we have are all theories. They are not far from being accurate. However, theories need not be the complete truth. We could go wrong at some time or at some points.

'We have no other option but to go ahead with our plans based on the theories which we have formed till now. So you have to plan for a trip to Sarawak and see what happens to your souls when you stay in the area where the two of you were born. Mansour will also come with you for any assistance.

I am very hopeful that once the two of you get recharged with your own positive-energy souls, the desert genies cannot affect you. Mansour can stay away from Dubai to work in Turkey. He will not have any further botheration from the desert negativity.'

Mansour had his own concerns. 'Grandfather, do we have to carry any specific tools or kit to fight the negative souls?'

Mahmoud smiled. 'You are thinking in line with Professor Van Helsing while he was encountering Count Dracula. There they use holy water, garlic, and crucifix to drive away the evil spirits. The energies from the souls I am talking about have nothing in common with the evil spirits. These are the antimatter, which is available in the space beyond our sensitivity and sight. They are the ones which, for millions of years, had been entering the human body and leaving these bodies when the time comes. This is the law of human life.

'The only way to counter them is to be stronger in mind and to have concentration on things which you want to do and achieve. Wherever you are, you should be aware of things happening around you and should observe very carefully to absorb the implication of things around you.'

Mansour had one more concern. 'What about the way Damla acted while she saw us at the sema? What could have caught hold of her to make her rush towards us?'

'This was the act of the negative energy which had entered Damla while she was in the desert. The positive part, which was in resonance with San, was urging her to meet San, whereas the negative part was pushing her to go to Mansour. The negative soul had tried in vain to enter Mansour when he was in the Dubai dunes. But the clever soul found Damla to be an easy prey and entered her partly and was pushing her to go to Mansour.

'When she met both of you together at the sema, her clear mind recognized you as the same persons that she had met in the desert camp. But then the fight started between the negative and positive energies. Luckily for all of us, Damla's positivity prevailed in spite of all the chaos she created at the hall.' Smiling broadly, Mahmoud turned towards Damla. 'Do you know how many persons got injured yesterday at the hall due to the stampede you created?'

Damla slowly shook her head to indicate her ignorance.

'From what I could understand from the caretaker of the hall, twelve people were taken to the nearby clinic to be given first aid. Others escaped with minor cuts and bruises. But nobody realized what the actual cause of the panic was. So, Damla, nobody will come in search of you. Have you talked to your parents about all this?'

Damla again shook her head. 'No, Uncle. I was not in a mindset to explain anything to my parents. I don't think they would ever understand this theory about antimatter and energies from the souls. They might think of taking me to a psychiatrist.'

'Okay, that's fine. How you will explain your trip to Sarawak with Mansour?'

'I have an idea.' I wanted to tell them what had flashed in my mind. 'Damla can tell them that she wants to revisit her place of birth and would like to go with her friend. Mansour would be an ideal boyfriend for Damla.'

Mansour jabbed me on the ribs. He had been trying to establish a love story between Damla and me. Now I could turn the cart on him. But in truth, I had felt that Mansour and Damla could be a made-for-each-other pair. Even though Mansour objected in the beginning, eventually he acceded to my suggestion. Mahmoud also thought that would be a good idea to convince Damla's parents.

I asked Damla, 'A honeymoon before the marriage—is that okay with your parents?'

Damla quipped, 'As I had told you before, my parents are not so orthodox. And Mansour being the grandson of the great Mevlana makes it all the more easier to make them agree to the trip.'

Mahmoud raised his right hand. 'My dear daughter, I am not the Mevlana. I am only a humble disciple of the great Mevlana. Calling me the Mevlana would be bringing the great Jalaluddin Rumi to a lower berth. Please do not compare me to the great Mevlana.'

'But, Uncle, you look exactly like the great Mevlana. My parents used to tell me about you, and all the Konyans believe that you are the real reincarnation of Rumi. It is not only the looks. Your deeds are also similarly honourable. We all love you so much, Uncle.'

'Okay, okay, dear Damla. Let us leave it at that. You can call me whatever you want. You are such a nice kid.'

I wanted to tell them my plans. 'Tomorrow I return to Sohar via Dubai. Then I have to check when my daughter can get some time off to travel with us to Sarawak. I intend to take my wife, daughter, and son with me for the trip. They had been looking forward to seeing the place where I had spent my childhood. For me also, a return to the stilted houses would be a dream come true.'

Damla was amused. 'We too were staying in a stilted wooden house. In front of the house there was a road, and beyond the road there used to be the forest.'

'We were staying in a similar place. The forest was not of large trees. It was full of very tall grass. The local tribe of the Dayaks lived deep inside the forest. We even had a local servant-maid by the name of Sari, who used to look after me in those days. I remember that I had loved her so much.'

'It seems that in twenty years, not much has changed in Lutong. Your childhood and mine seem to be almost similar. When we go there, maybe more similarities may arise. It would be really fun to see those places again and relive our childhoods.'

Mahmoud intervened. 'That would be a great reunion with your old friends if you can find them in Lutong. Now let us plan for the trip. Mansour, you should take Damla back to her house, and that will give Damla a chance to introduce her boyfriend to her parents. No need to tell them the plans for the trip immediately. It can be done later. Meanwhile, let them understand Mansour and get confident about him. That way, they will not feel sceptic about sending their daughter on a long trip with him.'

Mansour nodded. 'That's right, Grandfather. I agree with you. Okay, San, see you soon. You start packing up, and meanwhile, I will drop Damla off and return.'

We broke off the meeting. Damla and Mansour went out to Damla's house. Mahmoud retired to his room, and I went to our room to pack.

My mind was going over the incidents of the last few days. The world seemed so small. Meeting a person from the same place after such a long time was indeed a super coincidence.

I was very keen to make that trip to Sarawak with my family. It would be such a nice feeling to see all those places which are hidden in my memories. That reminded me to talk to my elder sister and brother to get some details of the family of Sari, our maid in those days. There must be some photos of Sari and her family members. I should remember to take these photos with me. Maybe there would be somebody who would be able to help me in finding them. Of course, it is highly unlikely that Sari would still be alive. But it was better to hope for the best. I did remember her as a very loving person allowing me to do so many mischief during those days.

I remembered what Mahmoud had told us regarding getting assistance from local residents. Therefore, getting to know the family of Sari would be a great help in our quest for re-energizing our souls. If by any miracle, Sari is alive, then she should be at least in her eighties. If I could meet her again and relive my childhood days, that would make my day!

I had planned for a peaceful, happy holiday in Sarawak with my family and my two new friends. But I could never have guessed what was in store for us.

CHAPTER 18

The Preparations

I was back in Sohar.

The last week was hectic. So many things had happened with our trip to Konya. The new place had given varied experience. Knowing Mahmoud was the best memory I had carried back with me. Such a learned man! Talking to him instilled so much confidence in me.

When I embarked on the trip to Konya with Mansour, I was not so sure that I could get out of this trouble from the desert. But now I was very confident that everything would come to a good end. We knew what the trouble was, and we had solutions to the problem as well. We were no longer in the dark about the cause of the mysterious events.

Mansour and Damla, being Turkish nationals, could enter Malaysia and Brunei without a visa in advance. They would be granted visas on arrival. But for us, since we were Indian nationals, getting visas in advance was a must.

Luckily, there were embassies for Malaysia and Brunei in Muscat. I made the visa applications for myself along with Jai and Kav. I advised Viv to get his visa in San Francisco. He would have no problems since the respective embassies were there as well.

I had to wait for Jai and Kav to come to Oman so that we could apply together for the visas.

Meanwhile, I planned for the trip. Our main destination, Miri, had an international airport. Even though there were no direct flights from Muscat or Dubai, there were daily flights from Singapore and Kuala Lumpur.

We decided to go via Singapore so that the flight selection would become easy. That meant one more visa to be applied for.

We had planned to stay in Miri. There were very good hotels. I had to select a medium-rated one. The trip to Seria in Brunei would be done by road. We could rent a car and drive to Lutong from Miri, which was about twenty kilometres along the coastal highway. From Lutong, it is about fifty-six kilometres to Seria, and we had to cross the border on the way.

Possibly, a one-day stay in Seria would be sufficient to get to know things as required for the purpose of our trip. It was important that we spend time in Miri and Lutong to find the roots of my soul. The same was applicable for Damla. Damla was to find out from her parents where she was conceived and born.

As Mahmoud had emphasized, we were to concentrate on the areas where we were conceived and born and where we were living during our childhoods. Once I know the place where my parents had stayed, the area where the conception had taken place would be known. That was a premium requirement to get our souls rejuvenated.

So my program was to stay in Singapore for a day and then fly to Miri. One week in Miri should be good enough to satisfy our souls as well as to satisfy the aim of the others in the trip, which was mainly sightseeing. During the one-week stay in Miri, we could make the trip to Seria and back by road.

If everything went as planned, we should be able to conclude our trip on a happy note, with our souls recharged with the much-needed positive energies from the source. Then all our worries could be put to rest. Kav would also be relieved.

I was in touch with Mansour to apprise him of the developments in the preparations for the trip. Apparently, he had struck a good chord with Damla's parents and was now a daily visitor to their place. Damla's parents were happy to welcome this handsome young man who was related to the great Mahmoud. They concluded that their daughter had selected well.

After my departure from Konya, Damla never had any problems like what she had experienced during the sema. So it was all peaceful and quiet for them.

I got all our tickets booked—Muscat to Singapore and, from there, to Miri—on Singapore Airlines. The rates were not too high. I conveyed the dates to Mansour so that they could make their bookings from Konya via Istanbul to our destination. Viv would land in Singapore from San Francisco at a time almost similar to ours.

We had almost a month to get prepared for the trip.

Meanwhile, I made arrangements for Jai and Kav to come to Muscat. The three visas would take almost two weeks to get issued since each embassy required three to four working days to issue the visa.

As usual, Jai and Kav reached Muscat by their Jet Airways flight, and I brought them to Sohar. The next day itself, we started the process of applying for visas from the three embassies.

Since they were in Sohar, Jai suggested going to Dubai for a couple of days so that they could make the entry to Dubai to keep their resident permits valid.

I felt it was a good idea, and we planned to make the trip during the weekend once we got our passports back from the Malaysian embassy.

At the outset, the trip to Dubai was a simple one, just like the many trips we had made in the past several years. But unfortunately, it turned out to be sour, and the past came haunting us once again.

We had left Sohar on a Friday morning. Somehow, Kav was not very keen on the trip. She suggested crossing the border and returning to Sohar from Hatta. She said she would love to stay at the Hatta Fort Hotel for a day. I could sense an inkling of fear in her attitude. She did not want to cross the desert safari area in Madam. She still had a fear that something untoward could happen if we go near that place.

But Jai wanted to go to Dubai to visit our cousins. They had recently moved from Chennai to Dubai. That was a reasonable request, and we had to relent to her suggestion. Reluctantly, Kav too agreed to go to Dubai.

I was driving at a very easy pace, and we reached the desert safari range by around eleven in the morning. We talked about the last trip we had made to the desert safari and relived the moments. Jai took the opportunity to pull my leg, citing the dancing incident.

Then suddenly, a loud cry came from Kav. She was pointing to the sand dunes on the left side of the road, which were rather higher than other dunes.

We too looked in the direction and were awestruck with the sight in front of us. I stopped the vehicle towards the side.

A Prado SUV had overturned and was tumbling down the sand dune. People from all around had started running towards the area where the accident was happening.

Looking at the tumbling car, I could see to my horror the shapeless entities by the side. What I had seen during the desert drive last time came back to me. I rubbed my eyes and looked again. No, those forms were there. One of them was trying to push the vehicle further, and the other was trying to stop the vehicle from tumbling again. It was obvious that the negativity was far stronger than the positivity.

Finally, the car came to rest on its back at the foot of the sand dune. By that time, many people had gathered around the car, trying to help the passengers.

Kav shouted loudly, 'Dad, please go away from this scene. I don't want to see any more of this. What we saw itself will not go away from my mind.'

Jai also pushed me to go forward rather than staying there. I was trying to see what the shapeless entities were up to.

I had the fright of my life when I saw that one of them had started moving towards us. It had reached the fence on the left side of the road. I was really panic-stricken now. My foot pressed the accelerator, and the car shot forward.

Kav cried out, 'Dad, please be careful! You don't have to rush like this.'

I could sense that Jai was looking at me in a puzzled way. She must have been wondering what had got into me. I thought that it was good that only I had seen those things. Otherwise, it would have been so confusing for Jai and Kav.

I looked in the rear-view mirror. There was nothing behind us. I turned my head to look behind. No, nothing was following us.

None of us talked for some time. I was thinking of the negative-energy concept. That thing had recognized me and was trying to reach me. I had escaped just in time. But there was the danger of this negativity when we return. I had to think of another road to use to go back to Sohar without raising any alarm in Jai and Kav.

The accident was gruesome. With the way the car was tumbling down, I was sure that it had been fatal to some of the passengers. The incident made me realize that it was not only me that these negative energies were pursuing. They had many other victims as well. Mahmoud's theory of the bad blood bringing negative energies was being proved beyond any doubt.

I had to be careful, and it was all the more important that we make our trip to Miri at the earliest.

We went directly to Bur Dubai, where our cousins were staying. By the time we reached Bur Dubai, Kav and Jai had cooled down. We never spoke about the incident in the car. All were visibly shaken, and nobody wanted to relive the accident by discussing it. I too thought that was better and resigned myself to the analysis of the spectre I had seen.

The negative soul was really powerful in the desert. The desert must be holding more negativity than positivity. It was obvious that the positive souls in the desert were much weaker in comparison to the negative ones. Even though the fights and the wars were of the past, the bad blood which had flowed during those days had been too much for the good deeds of the present generation to negate them. Therefore, it might take years and years to balance out the good with the bad and suppress the negativity forever.

I had got myself embroiled in this tussle for supremacy between the negative and positive souls. Luckily for me, Mahmoud was on my side, and that thought alone was enough for me to think more positively.

The return to Sohar could pose another problem. If we had to avoid the desert section, we had to go through Al Ain or take the eastern expressway to Fujairah. The trip through Al Ain would entail slow stretches inside the city before crossing over the border to Buraimi. The distance would increase by around forty kilometres and the travel would consume more time.

The eastern expressway through Fujairah would also have a similar effect. Apart from the distance, the border post at

Kalba is so slow that you waste a lot of time just for stamping the exit.

But how could I explain the change of plans to Kav and Jai? They would not fall for any excuse for taking a circuitous route. There was also no point in making them panic.

Maybe I should take a risk and shoot through that section of the road where the sand dunes lay on the two sides of the highway. After thinking a lot about the alternatives, I decided to take the same way back. I should be very alert and should pass the desert section within the shortest time possible.

Once I took the decision, I became relaxed. I started talking to Jai and Kav about other things we should do in Dubai during this trip. They too participated in the discussion animatedly. We decided to visit the Dubai Mall and, if possible, go to the top of Burj Khalifa.

That evening, we had a pleasant trip to the top of Burj Khalifa. The sight from the top was fantastic. It was like conquering Mount Everest to be at the highest point in the world. It would take days to reach the summit of Everest. But here we had reached the top within seconds inside a lift moving at a very high speed.

The sights inside Dubai Mall were enthralling, and the view from the top of Burj Khalifa was superb. We had a feeling of accomplishment. To top the day off, we had the chance to see the musical fountain in front of Burj Khalifa. We enjoyed the music as well as the dancing water fountains.

After dinner at the food court at the mall, we returned to Bur Dubai.

My fear of crossing the desert the next day came back during the night. I made up my mind to travel very early in the morning so that there would not be any crowd in the desert areas. Normally, they start to gather in the afternoon.

Hopefully, my enemy should be coming out with the crowd. It could not be having an intuition of my driving along its way.

So we left at eight thirty in the morning and went back to Sohar.

Chapter 19

Miri, My City

I had thought that one month was too long a period. But the days went by so fast that it was almost time for our travel to the Far East.

We had made a change in our plans for the travel. Earlier I had made our reservations from Muscat to Singapore. It was Jai who gave the idea to travel from Kochi to Singapore rather than them coming back to Muscat for this trip. This made sense. We could avoid the back-and-forth trips between Kochi and Muscat. So I made the booking for them from Kochi to Singapore and took an additional ticket for myself to travel from Muscat to Kochi.

I had talked to Mansour in between. Everything was going smoothly for both of them. Damla was away for a few days since she wanted to meet her uncle and aunt in Istanbul before making the trip to Malaysia. Mansour informed me that Damla had been preparing very well for the trip. She had gathered a lot of photos taken during their stay in Lutong. These photos would definitely help us in identifying many places and maybe to get in touch with some of the old friends of Damla's parents.

I too had some very old photos, but these dated back to the sixties. It was unlikely that the people in them were still around. It would have been best if I could locate the family of our old maid-servant, Sari. That would be a fantastic discovery.

Sari's children and grandchildren should be there somewhere. Being locals, they would be a great help in moving around the city to find our old buildings.

I remembered what Mahmoud had told us about getting the help of the local tribes. These were the people with the souls of the oldest positive and negative energies. They could be very useful in case something untoward happens. During my evening walks, my mind was in constant search for ideas on how to locate the kith and kin of Sari.

Fortunately, our trip from Dubai back to Sohar was uneventful. The idea of starting early really worked very well. There were no signs of any shapeless entities on the way. That was a big relief for me.

But while crossing the area where Kav had played with the proud peacock, we could see a crowd of ten to twelve people gathered around the shops. For a moment, I thought I saw somebody resembling Damla. When the car was passing by, this lady looked in the direction of the road. For a fleeting second, I saw the face of the lady, and my mind queried what Damla was doing here. Did I see a shapeless entity beside her? I was not sure.

During that fleeting moment, though that lady could not have seen me driving past, still I felt that her face bore a grin as though she recognized me at that distance. She was grinning as though she was saying, 'I will take you later.'

But coming to think of it, I knew I must have made a mistake in thinking it was Damla. There was no chance of Damla being there when she was roaming around Konya with Mansour. Maybe, as they say, when you think of somebody, all faces around may resemble that somebody. This too could have been a case of thinking too much of the same people. If it had been a man turning his head towards us instead of this lady, maybe I would have thought it was Mansour.

I did not give much importance to the event. We were actually much relieved that the return journey was peaceful. In order to satisfy Kav, we had a brunch at Hatta Fort Hotel. But this time she was not very particular about the hotel as she had been while we were on our way to Dubai. However, we had to have our food, and we had it at this beautiful hotel.

Within another week, we got the Brunei and Singapore visas, and the mission was completed for Jai and Kav. During that weekend, they took their flight back to Kochi.

The great day arrived, the day I would reach my hometown, and we started packing for the trip to the past. That time I did not realize that it was virtually going to be a trip to the past.

Viv had reached Singapore a day in advance, and informed us that he would be at the airport to receive us.

But Mansour gave us bad news. They will reach Miri a couple of days late. They had some problems which he had to settle. He promised to share with me the details when we meet in Miri.

That would give us two clear days to move around Miri as real tourists, which suited us well. I hoped that the problems faced by Mansour were not serious.

The next night, we boarded the Singapore Airlines flight from Kochi to Singapore. The flight was very pleasant, and in four hours, we were landing at Changi International Airport in Singapore, one of the world's busiest airports.

Viv was waiting for us, and we sailed through the formalities pretty fast. Meeting Viv after a long time was a thrill for us. He used to have a handsome moustache, which was no longer there. He had shaved it off to suit the general trend in the US. Physically, he had trimmed down, which proved his workouts in the gym to be useful.

The stay at the place of Jai's sister was uneventful. There was no time for going around for sightseeing since our flight to Miri was on the very next day at noon.

Finally, we landed at Miri International Airport in the afternoon. Even though Miri was supposed to be an international airport, we had to do the immigration formalities at Kuching. For this purpose, there was a stopover at Kuching for about an hour.

We had reached the city which I had been dreaming so much to be in—the city of my childhood! In those days, it was a rather small town. But now it had developed so much that recently the old town was granted the status of a city.

We had booked in Mega Hotel, which was next to the Soon Hup Shopping Complex. I had selected this hotel so that at leisure time we can just walk around the mall. The main attraction of the city centre was the City Fan. The hotel was just twenty minutes from the airport, and the City Fan was almost at a strolling distance.

The City Fan had been developed by the city council in the shape of a huge fan. Inside this area, they had created many gardens with an amphitheatre at the centre. Towards the left of the theatre were the botanical garden and the Islamic garden. To the right were the Chinese garden and the formal garden.

There was a musical fountain in front of the theatre and an IT library behind. The public swimming pool at one corner and the promenade at the entrance of the fan completed the beautiful City Fan.

We got really enthralled by the beauty of this place when we visited this area in the evening. There were plenty of restaurants of different styles, which made dinner very easy.

Since we had been travelling for the last two days, we decided not to stay up late into the night. But before retiring to bed, we discussed the places to visit the next two days.

The tourist information centre had given us the leaflets of the main attractions in the city. None of us wanted to have a running spree around all these places. When we visit these places, we should see them properly and understand the significance of each place. We decided to judiciously select the places to be visited so as to reduce travel time and increase sightseeing time.

On the first day, we planned to visit the Niah National Park, which was at a distance of eighty-two kilometres from the city centre. The second day could be devoted to places which were closer to the city centre.

For the second day, we planned to see the Lambir Hills National Park, which was situated within thirty-four kilometres from the hotel. If we leave Lambir after lunch, we should be able to cover Canada Hill, which was next to the very first oil well known as the Grand Old Lady and Taman Awam, a family park hardly six kilometres from the hotel. Dinner could be combined with shopping at the Tamu Muhibbah market.

The above visits would allow us to cover a good lot of beautiful spots in Miri. One important spot which we would not be able to cover was the Gunung Mulu National Park. Mulu is approachable only by plane. This would call for a day's stay at Mulu so that we could see the huge national park fully. It was more of a mountain trail which goes over a large area of the rainforest. Many caves were there, and the limestone pinnacles of Mount Api would have been a sight to behold.

We would see the video of Mulu for the time being and concentrate on the nearby places till the time Mansour and Damla arrived.

The next morning, we started early, immediately after breakfast, to Niah National Park. Viv, who was an ardent driver, was at the wheel. He enjoyed driving the car and was adept at following the directions on the GPS. I would not have been able to use the GPS and still concentrate on the road. In Oman, we never required any GPS to find places. The roads were so easy with no complications.

We were travelling at medium speed so as to enjoy the beauty of the city and the sides of the highway. It took almost an hour for us to reach our destination.

We had to agree that it was worth coming all this way to Niah to see this treasured national park. We had to cross a narrow river by boat. The warning sign 'Beware of Crocodiles' would have made anybody jittery, but fortunately, we saw no crocodiles.

Just near the jetty, there was an archaeological museum giving details of the Niah caves. From there, it was a neat trek of three kilometres to the mouth of the cave.

Going around the Niah caves was an experience which we would never forget. It is actually a complex of caves, many of them scattered around. Some are very deep and dark inside, emanating that sepulchral feeling of fear and horror. It bodes evil, which would have existed years ago when the barbaric tribes of headhunters and ferocious animals roamed the earth's surface.

The Kain Hitam, or the painted cave, which was located to the south of the main cave, is an ancient burial site, and the walls of the cave are filled with paintings carved on the limestone rock. All these came under the archaeological society's care and security. They had preserved the caves wonderfully well.

I was so preoccupied with the beauty of the caves and their paintings that I did not notice that I had wandered away from my family members and other tourists. I was almost alone in the painted cave. I saw a mount at one corner of the cave and approached it to check what it was. As per the information given by the centre, this should be one of the human burial places dating back to 40,000 years.

I touched the mount at the top and suddenly felt the cave revolving around me. Or was it that I was revolving around the cave? I was not sure what had happened to me. Several scenes were moving very fast in front of me. It was as though I was inside a cinema hall. The screen in front of me had several frames moving at a speed that confused me and never gave me a chance to understand what it was. I felt almost dizzy and thought I would be falling down.

I could remember seeing many ancient places with a number of faces, sometimes cruel and sometimes sympathetic, among hordes of people and beasts. Loud voices called out in a tongue I could not recognize, but they seemed familiar to my mind. It was as though I was living through those scenes. My final recollection was a sword being thrust towards me, and then I took my hand off the mount.

When I woke up, Jai, Viv, and Kav were around, and they were pushing and prodding me to wake me up from my faint. They were frightened to see me lying down in a stupor, and I was surprised to see them with their grave faces. I could not recollect anything immediately.

I told them that I had passed out briefly. They were worried that maybe my blood pressure had gone up with the stress of travel. After pacifying them that I had no problem at all, we went out of the caves. On our way back, I got time to reflect on the events which had led to me passing out inside the cave.

I felt it was strange that such scenes should come to me as though I was present during those events. The background of the scenes, which were almost blurred for me, related to some ancient era. I was trying to recollect all the visions I had so that I could reconstruct the events to get some logic from it. Were these also part of my theory of spinning into oblivion?

During the journey back to the city centre, I decided to share my experience with my family so that we all would be together in this and would be able to help one another in case of any emergency situation.

I was lost in my thoughts, and the others did not want to disturb me. And then it happened. While negotiating a turn, Viv was a little on the high speed and had to cut away from the car in front, which was at a lower speed on the speed track, to avoid a possible collision. In between the sudden turn of the car and the braking effect, I saw them on the road between the car in front and ours—the two shapeless shapes just similar to the ones I had seen in the Dubai sand dunes. For a moment, I panicked and almost cried out. But luckily, no sound came out of my throat since it had gone bone dry.

Once we passed the car and Viv smoothed the drive, the apparitions also vanished. But my worry was that the negativity was following me. Something had to be done urgently so that these nightmarish visions will cease to loom in front of me. It became all the more necessary that we discuss at length on the course of action to be taken so that we can share with Mansour and Damla as they join us on the morrow.

I stole a glance towards Kav. Did she see the apparition on the road? I was hoping it did not happen to her. I did not want her to be intertwined in this dream I had been following—or rather, had been following me. But her face did not give away her emotions. Maybe she did not see anything. If she had seen them, she would have been the first one to give a cry. I felt calm.

We had planned to have lunch at Niah. Even though it was already late in the afternoon, due to the sudden change of events, we had to leave the cave site before lunch. So on the way, we stopped at a food joint and relaxed. It was also good for Viv to get a break from the pressure of driving after that near mishap on the road.

CHAPTER 20

Search For Familiar Souls

The children got used to the Malay food very fast. But for Jai and me, we had to search for our vegetarian stuff. Anyway, nowadays so many people are turning into vegetarianism; it was not a problem to get food to our taste.

We relaxed around the table after a good lunch and savoury dessert to go with it. Till then all were concentrating on the food, and nobody talked about the events of the past. I decided to break the silence.

'I have to tell you something that I had been keeping to myself. Kav knows some part of it. Since I had been hoping that everything would turn out well fast, I did not want to pull you into these problems.'

I looked at the other three. Kav was keeping a sullen face. Jai and Viv raised their faces, surprised.

Viv was the first to react. 'What are you talking about, Dad? What problems do you have, and why you have not told us before? If Kav knows about it, you should have shared the facts with us earlier.'

I had to confront them. 'Listen, Viv. It was not a big problem to start with. I tried to solve it myself. But the recent events here proved to me that it is not something which I can escape from that easily. So I decided to tell you, and I will start from the beginning.'

They all listened to me intently, and I went on to describe all the events from the very beginning, starting with my strange dreams and the article I had written in the magazine.

It was like a flashback in the movies. Since I had thought of all these events and discussed with Mansour and Mahmoud about these happenings many times, it all came to me very easily scene by scene. The three of them just sat there listening to me and never interrupting me during the narration.

I ended my story with the rolling of scenes in the cave and the apparitions which appeared to me on the road.

Nobody talked for a couple of minutes even after I had stopped talking. It was as though they were trying to assimilate the facts almost stranger than fiction. I thought, *Maybe they think I had gone bonkers staying alone in Sohar for such a long time.*

But then Kav came to my rescue and told them what she had felt those days after reading my article and what she had seen in the desert during our safari.

I hoped Kav's assertion gave more credibility to my story. Jai was looking at Kav and me with full curiosity. She was one lady who took everything practically and never succumbed to fantasy rolled out of superstition. She was God-fearing and very pious, and she never let impracticality overrule her senses.

'San, I had been thinking that you had not been taking your tablets for BP, and that was why you had that dizziness inside the Niah cave. And of course, that day in the desert camp, I was almost laughing when you made yourself look clumsy by falling off the dance floor. Never thought there was really something which pushed you. I am still a little dazed from what I have heard now.'

I asked Kav whether she had seen the apparitions on the road where Viv had smartly veered off from the other car. No, she had not seen them. It was perfectly normal for her and nothing like what had happened in the desert.

I wanted to clear one more doubt with Kav. 'What about the day we were going to Dubai when we saw the Prado come tumbling down from the hilltop? Did you see any apparitions?'

'No, I did not see anything. But I was afraid from the accident. We were lucky that nothing had happened to us like that when we did the dune-bashing.'

That made me more relaxed. It was good that Kav was no longer affected by these things of negativity. As Mahmoud had explained, by being in the area of positivity for longer periods, her soul must have got recharged with enough positivity. Now the negative thoughts were not occurring to her. That made me the only one who needs to be recharged to get out of this muddle.

Viv, who had been silent till now, took over. 'Father, all these seem to be more fantasy than fact. I am not able to digest what you had been narrating. I am not inclined to believe that energy can appear in the form of apparitions. It was as though you had seen some English horror movie and were reliving the sequences from the movie in your subconscious mind.'

I knew Viv was agnostic and always trusted his own sense of righteousness. He formed his own opinion about anything connected to him.

'Viv, you know very well that I too think in the same way as you think about these so-called mystical happenings. But for me, what started as a benign dream had more ramifications than I could fathom. The series of events which had taken place subsequent to my dreams made me change my mind. I had to believe in them because it was affecting my life, and I had to come out of this situation somehow.'

Viv was not convinced. 'I do agree with the existence of positive and negative energies. At certain situations, we may feel the effect, but seeing it is next to impossible.'

'That is exactly why I took great pains in going with Mansour to meet his grandfather, a learned man. I am now convinced that I should follow his advice. Anyway, we do not have to do anything out of the way.'

Viv nodded in the affirmative. It seemed he had decided to play along with me. 'Okay, I agree with you. Let us go with the assumption that what Uncle Mahmoud had said is correct. Then it seems you have not reached where you had been conceived as yet. The idea of this trip for you was to get your soul recharged with positivity from the original source as suggested by Uncle Mahmoud. As per his knowledge, your soul should get automatically replenished when you travel around the area which is important for you. Looking at the events which had happened now even after roaming around Miri for two days, these point to the fact that your soul is still undercharged. So we have to find the exact place where your origin lies.'

'How do we find that out now?' I had no clues to offer immediately.

'You had been saying that you were born in Seria. Maybe we should go there.' It was Jai who questioned me about my knowledge about where I was really born.

'I was born in Seria in the hospital. But that doesn't mean that that is the place where the origin is. We should know where my parents were during those days. To my knowledge, we were in Miri and Lutong since father was working with the Sarawak Shell Oil Company in Miri. They must have taken mother to Seria for the delivery since the hospital was good over there,' I explained to her what I knew about our earlier life in Miri.

Viv came out with a suggestion. 'Father, all these areas where we are roaming around are newly created or modernized old places. We should go around some old places in Miri and see how the ambience affects you. Let us look at the map which the information centre had given us to find the places.'

Then Kav opened up. 'No need to look at the map. The Grand Old Lady should be the first place to visit. That is the first oil well and was a place of interest to all. The oil well is on Canada Hill, which overlooks the entire Miri City. Let us go there and see what happens.'

Viv immediately agreed with Kav, and we left the restaurant.

All were in a better mood than when we entered the restaurant for lunch. I too felt very good after opening up with them about the issues I was facing. Now I could discuss with them, and I could lean on to the ideas of three more brains.

Canada Hill was a limestone ridge overlooking Miri City and offering excellent views of Miri and its surroundings. The Grand Old Lady is the first oil well in Malaysia; it is situated on top of Canada Hill. The oil well was no longer in production and was now protected as a national monument by the Malaysian government.

We went to the observatory platform, from where we could get the overall view of Miri City. Even though Petroleum Museum was nearby, that did not create any interest in us since our present mission was something else other than sightseeing.

We walked around the place and then looked around to see far and wide of the city of Miri and beyond. As I was looking towards the eastern side of the city, over the road leading to Lutong and further towards Seria, I felt a twitch in my eyes. Somehow, I could sense halos over these areas, which were absent on the western side of the city.

I asked Viv whether he felt any specific difference between the west and east. He did not feel anything unusual, and so it was with Jai and Kav. Then I told them what I could feel and specifically the trace of attraction towards the east, towards Lutong and beyond.

That time I noticed that Kav was talking excitedly over the phone. When she stopped talking, all of us looked at her quizzically.

'It is confirmed. Father, you were born in Seria in Brunei, and also your origin is the same place. Grandfather was working in Seria in those days, and it was only after you were born that they had shifted to Lutong. So we should be travelling to Seria to end this mystery.' Kav finished talking in one breath.

We were all surprised at how she could get all these details so fast. Then she told us that she had been talking to Aunt Shanti. It was clever of Kav to have remembered to make the call. While we were trying to make sense out of the nonsense, she used her common sense.

The information was a great relief for us.

'Tomorrow evening, Mansour and Damla will reach Miri. Then along with them, we can drive to Seria the day after tomorrow. Once we make that trip, if Mahmoud is correct, I should finally be back to normal,' I explained our general program to the rest. My search for familiar souls should be achieved within two more days.

We decided to visit the marketplace before returning to the hotel. Tamu Muhibbah was only at a distance of two kilometres from where we were staying. So that made it very convenient for us to see the local system of bargaining and selling goods.

The visit was a very good experience for us. We roamed around the marketplace for nearly two hours. Kav and Jai could buy some things to their liking as well.

This was the place where people of all races from the villages in and around the Miri region come to sell their foodstuff and buy what they lack in their places. The market was very lively, and we could spend some time forgetting all other apprehensions in our minds. The wide variety of fruits of different colours and shapes was a soothing sight for the eyes and mind.

Dinner was taken from the food park near the market. It was good to see these food parks, which offer different cuisines from all over the world. We could see a number of tourists gathering in the food park area and enjoying food that suited their palate. We could also get dishes to our liking.

Before retiring for the day, we debated on the places to visit the next day. After going through the information sheet we had with us, we picked Lambir Hills National Park for the morning session and Taman Awam, a family park, for the afternoon session. Lambir was thirty-four kilometres away from the hotel whereas Taman Awam was within six kilometres range. Distance-wise the two spots fit well with our plans. We wanted to be back at the hotel by six in the evening so that we get some time to spend with Mansour and Damla, who were slated to land around the same time.

The next day found us very fresh and ready for our adventure to Lambir Hills National park. Driving came very easy for Viv, whereas for me, it was not easy to drive vehicles I was not accustomed to. So it was Viv again behind the wheel, guiding us to our morning destination.

Lambir Hills was an ideal place for adventure lovers who find pleasure by indulging in jungle trekking, dipping in waterfalls, and sighting insects, wildlife, and plants. The advertisement on the park entrance welcomed us, telling us to be ready for the nature lover's dream-come-true experience.

The park had many trekking trails. But we were not prepared for making any trekking. Instead we spent our time enjoying the beauty of the diverse plant life. We were informed that there were 1,050 different types of trees in the park along with 1,200 species of insects.

The waterfall named Latak was a beauty. It cascaded from the Lambir Hill, forming a large pool at the bottom, where the trekkers were cooling themselves down.

Some of the flowers were really extraordinary. I doubted whether these flowers could be seen anywhere else in the world. We had always thought of seeing the rainforest, and we could really quench our curiosity. All around us were huge trees towering to the sky; there were many places where you could not see the sky at all. The greenery was enthralling.

We were not aware of the time until our empty stomachs started their drumbeats to announce that it was already time for lunch.

With a heavy stomach and cool, satisfied minds, we left the national park on our way to Taman Awam, the family park. On the way, Viv was very careful in not speeding up the car lest I get the unwelcome sight of my shapeless friends from the other side of oblivion.

We had debated a lot on the selection of the destination for the afternoon trip. Generally, the children were of the opinion that a family park would be a dreary drab like any other entertainment parks. But we finally settled on Taman Awam since it was very close to our hotel.

However, what awaited us at the park was something which we had not bargained for. The area was a very lively and colourful sight. The hustle and bustle of the park even at the afternoon time raised our spirits very high.

The suspension bridge over the water park, botanical gardens, jogging trails, stone carvings and sculptures, and the imposing wooden walkway over the road leading to the observation platform were a few of the attractions which we could see within the time available. The park covered a huge area.

After going through all the nearby entertainment spots, we paused in front of a kiosk to take some rest before thinking of the next step.

I could almost curse myself for having agreed to ride the dancing girl's skirt. I knew very well it was not good for my frame of mind to take an adventurous ride, but I succumbed to the taunts of my children and Jai. I did not want to be labelled a chicken by them, so I climbed on to the seat beside Jai, while Viv and Kav took another seat behind us. The ride, which was enjoyable for others, became a nightmare for me.

The start was a calm affair. The skirt picked up speed and started going up and down while moving sideways. I saw that others were happily screaming about and thought that I could also enjoy this seemingly simple ride myself. Then it happened.

Panic gripped me when my head started whirling around. I wanted to scream, but no sound came out. The pictures were right in front of my eyes, rolling away one by one at a high speed.

In the beginning, I could not make out anything from those pictures. The movement of the pictures or scenes was happening at a great speed. Then I realized that it was getting repeated, and the third or fourth time, I could make out something out of these pictures.

The first lot of pictures was just lights and banging sounds. Then there were green forests and many huge beasts roaming around. The scenes changed from animals to people who were like aborigines scantily dressed. They turned into ferocious men, killing one another and cutting off the heads of their opponents. Then there were many civilized people walking around, who soon were riding horses and fighting great battles.

Scenes kept changing rapidly, forests giving way to huts and then houses. Horses changed to vintage cars, and people were digging the earth while some black liquid poured out of these wells. Then there were aircrafts screaming in the sky, spitting fireballs. There were great fires all around that area, engulfing many a house and people. Suddenly, everything became calm, and ordinary people appeared from nowhere.

Then the complexion of the people changed from black-skinned to white-skinned through to brown-skinned, and finally, I thought I recognized some of the people in the scenes.

By the time I started realizing that there was some familiarity in the background of the dream sequence and that known faces were moving towards me, I must have lost consciousness.

The next thing I knew, Jai was prodding me to wake up, saying that the ride had ended and that we had to get out of the seats. She must have thought I was sleeping, and she commented on how I could sleep even when the skirt was going at such a rapid pace, moving up and down all the while. Dazed, I stepped out of the ring and on to the ground.

I tried to recollect what I had seen before it got erased from my memory bank.

It could have been a repetition of what I had experienced in the Niah caves the previous day. The only difference was that there I could not make out anything from the scenes that had appeared before my eyes, and here it was more cognizable and specific. It was as though I was being moved through the history of the place, a movie being shown at fast-forward mode.

It was a high-speed flashback.

CHAPTER 21

Return to the Birthplace

For the second day in succession, I was returning to the hotel midway of our trip as a casualty of my own imaginations. At least this time I had a very clear picture of what had gone through my mind.

I did not discuss the incident with my family since I wanted to ensure that the mental pictures remained firm in my mind before it got erased from my subconscious mind. This was very essential to analyze the situation in a better way.

When we reached the hotel, there was a message from Mansour, informing us that they were in the room adjacent to our room. That was great news. The important players in this whole drama had joined us in our search and research.

I called them through the intercom and invited them to have dinner with us in the hotel restaurant.

After a quick wash, all four of us reached the restaurant. Kav and Viv were looking forward to meeting this young Turkish couple that they knew through my narration.

Within half an hour, we all met in the restaurant. It was really heartening to see Mansour and Damla after a long time. Very soon, Viv became close with Mansour and Kav was talking animatedly with Damla. We sat at the dinner table, and they chose seats near one another.

We ordered our dinner. Each had specific taste, and a number of different dishes were soon seen on our table. While eating, I explained the incidents which had taken place after our reaching Miri. I took time to describe the scenes which had passed through my mind while riding the whirling skirt at Taman Awam.

The listeners were awestruck when I narrated the scenes. The question was why and how these scenes could or would appear in my mind. Most of the things had no connection with me other than the fact that I was born and had been living in these areas during the early stages of my life.

It was almost as though I was reliving the history of Miri. The summary of the history was fed to me in the form of a sphere around which I was sailing at a high speed.

Mansour started, 'It seems that your soul is a combo of the positive and negative energies of the souls which had existed in this area through the centuries. With your mind having been disturbed by the incidents in Dubai, it is now prone to be open to the souls of similar nature or part of your soul itself, which is on the other side of oblivion. The high-speed spinning of the skirt triggered the sequence to appear in front of you. Your theory of spinning into oblivion gains more sanctity with this occurrence.'

'I too support Mansour's analysis.' That was Viv, who had just finished gobbling up a piece of fried chicken leg. 'Mansour's idea makes a logical sense to our discussions till date. We should follow this so as to ensure that we fill up your soul with more similar positive energy before any negativity could capture the empty spaces within.'

'That makes our trip planned for tomorrow all the more important. The earliest we travel out the better. I could not hide my anxiety. 'Luckily, Seria is very close by, and we should be able to make it within an hour or so provided we get a smooth sail through the border check post.'

'Father, what about Damla?' That showed Kav's concern of her new friend. 'You all seemed to have forgotten that we have to get Damla's soul also recharged. She was the one who had more problems than what father was facing.'

Jai, who had been silent till now, joined the conversation. 'Damla, how do you feel after reaching your old home country? Any specific changes? Any visions or dreams like San was getting these days?'

Damla shook her head. 'No change at all. I feel perfectly well at present. Who knows when it will change! I know the place where we were staying during our days here. Once we come back from Seria, we can go to that area so that may be I too can get recharged. Any way I would like to see my old home and the neighbours. Maybe those people are still there, or maybe the recent modernization of the city have altered the whole landscape and its inhabitants.'

Mansour said conclusively, 'That settles it. Trip to Damla's hometown could be deferred till we come back from Seria. The important task at hand is to travel to Seria to find out what awaits us there.'

We changed our topic to nicer things, like sightseeing in Miri and a long-awaited trip to Turkey for my family. They had been talking about staying in Cappadocia. Mansour became very talkative when we switched the topic to his home country. Damla was not very much aware of the places in Turkey since she had spent most of her time outside the country. But Mansour had the advantage of listening to his grandparents, who had fed him the beauty and valour of the Turkish people.

It was late by the time we retired to our rooms. The children were very enthusiastic, looking forward to the trip on the morrow and also with the beautiful images of Istanbul and Cappadocia in their minds. The contended look on Jai's face mirrored her mind as well. Maybe I was the only one a little bit wary of what could be lying in ambush for us on our trip to Seria.

Seria was one of the major towns in the Sultanate of Brunei. It was developed with oil wealth. Shell had opened their oil wells in 1929 and had made the town grow. The sultan of Brunei was now one of the richest persons in the world. The country offered very high salaries to the expatriate workers who throng this area.

We had started our drive early in the morning. Our aim was to go around the town of Seria and then drive onwards to Bandar Seri Begawan, the capital of Brunei. Since we had come so far, it was not logical to return without seeing the beauty of the capital.

Seria was only sixty kilometres from Miri, and on the way, we passed the town of Lutong. We did not spend much time in this town since we had decided to come here later once we are back from Brunei.

The road was very well maintained, and it was a thrill for Mansour and Viv to drive on this road. They took turns at the wheel. We were driving along the South China Sea, and the natural beauty of the green tropical forests on the opposite side was enthralling. It reminded me of the drive we used to have from Ras Al Khaimah border to Khasab in the Musandam Governorate in Oman. There was the deep blue sea on one side and the barren mountains on the other side for a stretch of thirty-four kilometres.

The emigration checkpoint was at Sungai Tujuh about thirty kilometres from the Miri city centre. Once we crossed the Malaysian immigration point, we travelled straight over the winding roads to reach the Brunei immigration check post. We had our visas already stamped in our passports, and for Mansour and Damla, they just gave entry stamps. The whole process was over within minutes. The Brunei government was wooing more visitors to their country and hence had made the immigration procedures very simple.

We made it a point to go around the town of Kuala Belait and especially the old BMP hospital. That was the hospital where I was born, and even though I was not very sure, we must have somehow stayed in a house near the hospital. The whole area must have changed a lot. However, the more I was in the vicinity of this old town, the better I felt. Maybe it was a psychological effect of what Mahmoud had filled my brain with from all those talks we had in Konya. I strongly believed in Mahmoud's theory of the evolution of souls. That was our guiding light for getting to normal lives.

I was feeling very much elated since my mind was filled with images of positive energy of the souls around this place. Unknowingly, I was taking deep breaths as though to inhale the souls along with the fresh air around. Since I had no memory of having stayed in this town, nothing looked familiar to me. After spending half an hour around Kuala Belait, we drove towards Bandar Seri Begawan.

The capital was about 127 kilometres away from Seria. With a coffee break in between, we reached the beautiful capital of Brunei in time for lunch.

We had a quick lunch and then set off to see this beautiful capital city of Brunei. Everything was neat and orderly around. The roads almost sparkled, indicating that they were being cleaned very often. Like in the Middle Eastern countries, there must be cleaning companies contracted for maintaining the city's simple road systems and monuments. Our experience with Brunei proved that it was not only the capital which was taken care of by the government but also the suburbs like Seria.

Since we did not have much time with us, we decided to travel around the city to see the specific places of interest from outside rather than spending time to go inside to have elaborate sightseeing.

The Kampung Ayer consisted of twenty-eight villages on stilts. These are located on either banks of the river Sungai Brunei. During rainy season, water from the river floods the banks of the river, and the villages are virtually in water. Therefore, Kampung Ayer is also known as the Water Village.

We drove past the Istana Nurul Iman (the Palace of the Light of Faith), which is the official residence of the sultan. The surprising fact about this palace is that there are 257 bathrooms built in this place.

The Omar Ali Saifuddin Mosque is a wonderful work of architecture showcasing the sultan's love for art and preserving the culture. It was named after the twenty-eighth sultan of Brunei, who was the father of the present sultan.

We passed by many museums out of which the Brunei Museum and the Royal Regalia Museum were of much importance to the locals. Even the one-time residence of Britain's colonial-era high commissioners, which is said to be the sultanate's oldest extant building, is now a museum dedicated to the long-standing special relationship between Brunei and the UK. This museum is known as the Twelve Roofs House.

There were many more citadels of knowledge, like the Malay Technology Museum, Ratna Dina Arif Gallery, Kampung Ayer Cultural & Tourism Gallery to name a few. Due to shortage of time, we decided to circumvent all these places of common interest.

Finally, we reached Brunei's largest mosque, Jame'Asr Hassanil Bolkiah Mosque. The mosque has a special design to commemorate the twenty-fifth year of reign of the current sultan; it was built in 1992. The complex was adorned with twenty-nine golden domes since the sultan was the twenty-ninth in the dynasty. The four terrazzo-tiled minarets with its exquisite design dominated the overall look of the mosque from a distance.

Mansour wanted to go inside the mosque to offer his prayers. We all nodded our agreement. While he went inside, we lazed around the mosque to absorb its beauty. Damla was reluctant to go with Mansour. I felt it strange that Damla did not want to go to pray. As far as I knew, she was not an atheist. Then what was the reason for her reluctance? But when Mansour insisted, she went with him.

They did not spend much time inside. Mansour said the mosque was not crowded at all inside, and they could finish their prayers very fast. But later he confessed to me that Damla did not allow him to pray properly. She was insistent and adamant to go out fast. It was as though she was almost getting suffocated within the walls of the mosque.

By that time, it was getting late for us to travel back. The sun had gone to the west, leaving the skyline scattered with red and yellow streaks. It would soon be dark. It seemed that I was the only one who was concerned about driving in the night.

My worries were different. The darkness could bring back the effect of the shapeless entities on me or maybe on Damla as well. I was almost confident that I had got recharged with my positive souls—the peace of mind reflected a balanced thinking process—while travelling around Seria. But I did not feel the same confidence in the case of Damla. Her refusal to go inside the mosque marked some effect of negativity in her. We should try to reach Lutong before Damla's mind gets altered to the wrong end.

In case of any untoward happenings, our best bet would be to get inside the vicinity of Lutong, where Damla had her origins. Whether positive or negative, the main parts of her soul should be lurking in the area around Lutong similar to mine being in Seria. By trying to be closer to the places where good things had happened to her parents during those years, we could ensure positivity filling her mind and soul.

I was sure that my mind would not be at peace unless we reach Lutong.

My apprehensions proved to be correct with the events which took place while we were on our way back. Luckily, things started happening only after we crossed the border of Brunei into Malaysia. The two border posts were behind us when the first streaks of terror struck us.

CHAPTER 22

Embroiled in History

'STOP THE CAR!' The wild shriek almost made Viv veer off the car to the left bank of the road. But somehow, he kept control of the car and slowly pulled off to one side of the road.

I was a little bit sleepy when I heard the scream; it made me fully awake. I was sure both Jai and Kav would have got the shock of their life.

It was Damla who had cried out so loud. Mansour looked back to see what had happened to Damla. She kept blabbering something. What I could understand was that she wanted to get out of the car.

Since she was sitting near the window, the moment the car stopped, she opened the door and got out of the car. By the time Mansour got out from the front seat, Damla had started running.

All of us were so dumbfounded that we were unable to fathom the gravity of the situation. Only Mansour seemed to have regained his poise, and he ran behind Damla.

Darkness had started to settle all around us. But we could see the lights of Lutong very close in front. That was at least a bit of a relief under the circumstances. Damla was running towards the city.

Viv started the car and went behind the running figures in front of us. That was thoughtful of Viv. There was no point in all of us running behind Damla for whatever reason she had thought of doing such a thing. By the time we reached them, Mansour had got hold of Damla and was trying to pacify her.

My thoughts went awry. I had seen Damla running in the same frenzy in the sema hall in Konya. There she had later confessed to us that she felt as though some sort of energy was driving her to run. She had created such a panicked situation around that time that many people got hurt in the melee which had followed. Here at least nobody was on the road, and fortunately for us, no other vehicle was behind us. The situation could have been different if the traffic had been thick.

If one tended to believe Mahmoud, Damla should be craving for the recharge of her soul, which could have prompted her to go wild. So it was important for us to go inside the town of Lutong and take her to the place where she had been living with her parents long back.

Or it could be that more negativity had entered her soul, which was driving her mad at something or somebody.

As per Mahmoud's theory, everybody's soul comprised of both negative and positive energies. The villainous character of a person comes from the negativity of the soul, and positive energy imparts the graciousness of a person. The more the positivity, the better the person would behave.

My mind went a little bit wild.

Could it be that a similar situation existed while Mansour and Damla were in Konya, which had prevented them from travelling on the day we had actually planned?

Could it be that the figure I saw at the Dubai dunes while we were returning from our trip from Dubai was really Damla herself? Probably my doubts were correct.

Could there be more facts attached to the behaviour of Damla than what we knew till now? Could she be hiding some facts from us? Maybe her past in Lutong could have had some darker aspects.

She seemed to be telling the truth whenever we had encountered her from the beginning. If she had been hiding things, Mahmoud could have easily found them out with his sense of clairvoyance. He was closer to the evolution of souls than any of us, and his staunch belief in his theory would have aided him in finding out the whole truth from any person he met. This was what had assisted him in providing psychological counselling to many people in Konya. So Damla could not have kept any secrets away from Mahmoud.

My mind returned to the present when I realized that Mansour had managed to push Damla inside the car. This time he sat next to her, and Kav went to the front seat. I was in the extreme back seat and could not move out unless the front seat was lifted. At that time, I had a feeling of helplessness by being trapped between the seat and the back door. Without outside help, I could not come out of the car. That was a situation in which nobody would like to be in real life.

Damla was pacified, or that was what I felt. Once we started moving, I saw that she was again and again looking behind. I could not understand whether she was looking at me or beyond me. Her expression was almost a blank one as though she had nothing in her mind. But in spite of that bland expression, I could sense some sort of vengeance in her eyes.

Was she reliving her past in these areas? Maybe she had met somebody or just sensed the existence of somebody she loathed or rather her soul abhorred. Her negativity seemed to hold an upper hand compared to her positivity. We had to think of how to make her soul get recharged with positivity before the negative parts of her soul's past gained control of her mind.

At that moment, I wished fervently that Mahmoud was here with us.

Maybe that would not be a bad idea after all—requesting Mahmoud to join us immediately. Mahmoud would know better than us on how to control such things. Compared to him, we were just children in the nursery.

Jai, Viv, and Kav kept completely silent. They had come to like this girl so much that the sudden change in her personality had them wondering what to do next. Since Kav was sitting next to Damla, she must have panicked with Damla's behaviour.

By the time we crossed into Lutong, Damla had fallen asleep, with her head resting on Mansour's shoulders.

Viv turned his head towards Mansour to ask whether we should stop in Lutong. But Mansour told him to drive straight to our hotel in Miri.

We drove in silence since none wanted to disturb Damla in her sleep.

When we reached the hotel, Damla woke up. Even though she looked normal, she was rather tired. She seemed to have no memory of what had happened to her an hour back. So we decided to retire for the day and meet in the morning to decide our further plans.

My mind was rolling over the recent events, and with Damla's probing eyes in front of me, carrying an expression of vengeance boiling in her sharp eyes, I slipped into a deep slumber.

The whole town was agog about the ambush of the small army whom the sultan had sent to Miri to control the wayward Dayaks. The patrol party had comprised of twenty-five young men. The sultan of Brunei had got wary of the looting and killing of the people in Miri and around. Even though the Dayaks had stopped their habit of headhunting, they were yet to become civilized in the sense of living peacefully with others.

The news of the ambush made the sultan very angry, and he decided to send a full army to crush the culprits. But that would have led to a bloody war, and a lot of innocent lives would have been sacrificed. The internal minister's tactical mind prevailed over the sultan's rush for blood, and they decided to send Abdul Rehman, who was known to be a one-man army well versed in tackling grave issues of the state on his own.

Abdul Rehman had reached the village of the Dayaks in the attire of a peasant. By living with the Dayaks for almost a month, he understood that the so-called witch doctor of the clan, a woman by the name of Sera Seri, was the reason why the Dayaks were still rebellious and barbaric.

That day, the Dayaks found Sera Seri dead inside her bamboo hut, and the peasant who came from nowhere vanished from the village.

I woke up profusely sweating, and I felt that my throat had gone dry. I tried to recollect what I had been seeing. The figures in the dream were still dancing in front of my eyes. My mind was throbbing with the names Sera Seri and Abdul Rehman.

I could not understand why this strange dream had to come to my mind. It made no sense to me since these people had no connection with my life. Before thinking more about it, I got up to quench my thirst. The cool water from the refrigerator gave instant relief to my parched throat.

I went back to the bed since I did not want to startle Jai. Strange were the dream and the characters in it. But somehow I felt some closeness to them. Sometime during my life, or probably my past life, I must have encountered them.

Abdul Rehman came from Brunei, and Sera Seri lived in Miri. My origin was Brunei, and Damla was from Miri or Lutong. Was there a connection? The evolution of souls could have played its part in connecting the past to the present.

Could it be that Damla's vengeance was directed towards me? In Konya she had singled me out to be contacted. She had told us at that time that she had seen me in Dubai desert. Maybe it was more than that.

Maybe Sera Seri was hunting down Abdul Rehman!

I snoozed off with my mind full of dancing, screaming Dayaks.

The white rajah of Sarawak, James Brooke, was visiting the small town of Miri. Normally, he would stay in the capital of Sarawak, Kuching, where he had his palace. Therefore, the folks of Miri looked at his visit as an event to celebrate.

The white rajah was well liked by all the inhabitants of the town. But still there were some rebellious clans in the jungle who were yet to accept civilization. The sultan of Brunei had many problems with these tribes, and once James Brooke accepted his request for ruling Sarawak, he had some respite. James ruled with an iron hand to quell all rebellions. The country was brought back to normalcy, and the citizens learned to live in peace.

But there were some very dangerous elements from the local tribe Iban, who were roaming around the town of Miri and its surrounding areas to create unrest. They had planned to unsettle the celebrations for the day. They knew that they would not be able to reach the rajah with all his soldiers around him. But they could definitely create some commotion to divert the attention of the soldiers and thereby getting a chance to have a go at the persons closer to the rajah. Even one person killed would count many rewards from their chief.

The most ferocious among them was a woman by the name of Salamah. Even the men feared her wrath. She was always in the forefront in any sort of ambush or assault. She was now aiming at the rajah or at least one of his lieutenants. But she did not know how clever the Loyal Ring of the chief of

Miri was. The Loyal Ring, as it was known, was formed with the special soldiers sent by the sultan of Brunei. That was the help the sultan could give for the good governance of the state.

Miri, being very close to Brunei, had always been the speck in the eye of the sultan. So for him, the border areas needed to be peaceful for the development of his own country. The Loyal Ring was developed in Seria and loaned for the protection of the chief of Miri.

They had smelled the trouble brewing on the occasion of the rajah's visit and had trailed the mischiefmongers. Before the Ibans could mount their attack, the soldiers of the Loyal Ring found them out and cordoned off the ten people who were in the attire of country sellers. If they had surrendered, they could have had their lives spared. But the ferocious Ibans would never surrender, and they fought the soldiers. One by one, they lost their lives.

Abdul Lahiri, the master of the Loyal Ring, confronted the tricky Salamah. Since she was in the attires of a man, Lahiri never realized she was a woman. Only when she cried out when his dagger pierced her heart did he realize that he had committed a dreadful mistake by taking the life of a woman. It was too late by that time, and she lay in his arms, breathing her last. But the bluish dark eyes of Salamah stared at him as she uttered her last words. She was talking in her Iban language, which Lahiri could not understand.

That was the second time in the night that I got up from my sleep. This time, the words 'See you again' was vibrating in my head. I remembered what I had been dreaming. Again the characters were not at all connected with my life, or so I presumed. But the last words of Salamah were booming in my head. In the dream, she was talking gibberish, which nobody could understand. But in my mind, it became meaningful as though I had an auto-translator.

The seemingly unconnected events which appeared in my dreams were almost like they were happening in front of me. The only logical connection I could find after a long time of thoughtful sojourn was that in both events, a woman from Miri had been killed by a man from Brunei. The woman had been involved in heinous crimes, whereas the man was an avenger of the state.

From the location backgrounds, which I remembered clearly, the events had happened many years apart. The second part of my dream could have taken place at a more civilized circumstance than the first one, which means probably a century or half a century later.

Looking at it from the Mahmoud angle, the negative souls were far more prominent in the women, and the positive charges governed the men. While the positivity came from the more civilized Brunei during those times, the jungles of Miri offered proximity towards negativity.

The thought that I had my origin in Brunei and Damla had her origin in Miri or Lutong made me shudder. Could it be that she was wreaking vengeance on me? Were Salamah's last words coming true? 'See you again!'

I remembered those revengeful eyes looking at me in the car. At that time, I had thought that Damla was looking beyond me somewhere, searching for someone. Now, with a chill, I realized that she was aiming me.

How cleverly she lured me to her hometown from the deserts of Dubai!

Now what was the way to escape? How could we alter the negative character of Damla to a positive one so that she could forget the vengeance of Salamah and Sera Seri?

I could not sleep any more. I was afraid that more characters from the eventful history of Brunei and Miri might come haunting me. Sera Seri and Salamah were more than enough to spoil my peace for the next few days.

I had only one person to whom I could look up for help in this situation.

The time difference was almost seven hours. So he must be still awake. I took my cell phone and started dialling.

CHAPTER **23**

The Dayak Gardens

We met for breakfast. I was watching Damla, but she was as pleasant as ever. There were no traces of what had happened untoward yesterday. She seemed to have no memories of the turmoil she had gone through.

All others took care to act very normal with Damla lest she gets violent again.

'So what do we do today?' I started the dialogue so that we can decide on the program for the day. I had my own plans. But I did not want to present them in the beginning. It would look better if I put them across to them as though others suggested it. I should not give any chance to Damla to think that we, or rather I, was aware of her inner split personality. That could complicate issues.

'I am ready for anything.' That came from Viv.

'Me too, Dad,' Kav supported Viv.

I was hoping at least one of them to suggest what I had in mind. Both disappointed me. But then Jai came to my rescue.

'We have seen San's birthplace. But we are yet to see where this lovely Damla had lived with her parents in this beautiful city. My vote goes for Damla's dwelling!'

I sighed in my mind. That was a relief. Now we should understand where Damla had been living. There was a chance that if I had posed this question to her, she might act negatively, and maybe her inner personality would come out. Now that

Jai had proposed what I had in mind, I expected a positive response from Damla. My long-distance advisor could not go wrong.

All were looking at Damla. Initially, her face bore a blank look. But then it broke into a broad smile. Now she looked the same old pretty Damla.

'I was about to tell you that I want to visit my old house. In the past twenty years, several things would have changed. But it would be such a lovely experience to see the place.'

'Where is this place? Is it nearby, or do we have to go to Lutong?' That was Mansour at last opening his mouth.

'It is in Lutong. We were staying in stilted wooden houses. San knows about those houses. He was also staying in one of those. I think it could be the same area.' She paused to look at me. 'You said there was a jungle in front of your house. Our servant-maid used to tell me that there was a jungle in front of our place years before we came there. Most of the jungle areas were cleared to make the new township.'

'Then it must be the same place. But I do not remember the name of the place. I was only six when we left the place.' I was now bold enough to talk to Damla. We did not have to be afraid that she would break into another hysteria. She seemed to be past that stage at least for the time being.

'It is known as the Dayak Gardens,' Damla quipped. 'Since the jungle was earlier the home of the Dayaks, the government wanted to remind everyone that it belongs to the Dayaks and that they have a right to live among others. Many houses in that area were given free to the Dayaks as part of their rehabilitation process. Otherwise, we would have— sorry—they would have rebelled and made the lives of others miserable. But with the rehabilitation process in place, all are happy. They get lots of things at subsidized rates. That was how it was when we were living in the area in front of Dayak Gardens.'

Even though it could have been a slip of the tongue, I noticed that she had used *we* before changing it to *they* while talking about Dayak rebels. The subconscious mind would sometimes play lots of tricks on us. It was something like being unintentionally intentional.

At that time, my phone rang. I could see that it was a local number. I wondered who it could be. I did not want to make the others suspicious of my moves, so I asked them to excuse me since the call was from my boss in Dubai.

I took the call while standing outside the restaurant. It was a stranger. 'Are you San, the one who had put the photo in the *Morning Times*?'

I was happy that I could get a response to the advertisement I had inserted in the *Morning Times* single-page tabloid. I had posted the photo of Ahmed Bin Menser, who was the son of our old servant-maid Sari; I had carried it with me so that I could contact them somehow. I had remembered Mahmoud's words and thought that the local Dayak could be a source of enlightenment for the problems faced by us. It had such a fast response as luck favoured me.

'I am Altaf.' The person introduced himself. 'Ahmed Bin Menser is my father. It was nice to see my father's young face in the paper.'

I was thrilled to hear those words. But how come he saw the ad so fast?

'Altaf, good morning. It is so nice of you to have responded so fast. Even though I do not remember your father, I always used to think about your grandmother, Sari. She used to look after me when I was a child. How is she now, and how is your father?'

'My grandmother is very old. But she still has a sharp brain and eyesight. My father is okay, but he stays in the house. Both will be very happy to see you, San.'

'Where are you now? How and when can we meet with one another?'

'I work with the tabloid *Morning Times*. That was how I could see the ad so fast. You chose the right place to give the ad. You tell me where you will be, and I will go there to meet you.'

'We are staying at Mega Hotel. But now we will be moving towards Dayak Gardens. Can you meet us there? I have to talk to you as well. Later we can plan to see your father and my Sari.'

Altaf agreed to meet us in another hour at Dayak Gardens.

My mind was racing while I retraced my steps back to the restaurant. How should I utilize this opportunity to our advantage so as to get Damla back to be the positive-charged person? What Mahmoud had told me on the phone was reverberating in my ears. I had to play it casually and tactfully without raising even a small iota of suspicion in the mind of Damla. If she smelled anything, she can turn violent even without her own knowledge.

I smiled at the gang, who were devouring large chunks of bread, butter, and boiled vegetables along with chicken nuggets. I explained to them that the boss had called just to say hello and to check whether everything was going well for us in our vacation.

After deciding to meet within fifteen minutes at the parking lot, we headed towards our rooms.

The sight of the houses on stilts near the Dayak Gardens brought back memories of the sixties. This was the place where we used to make mock gang wars, using the long grass from the jungle as weapons shot from rubber bands kept between the thumb and the index finger. Even though the houses looked the same as in my memory, I could not place which one was our home in those days. The area had changed a lot with good roads all around and beautiful gardens in between the rows of houses.

I had a faint memory of how I used to go under the house on the stilts to escape from my mother. Nobody else could go through the small space between the floor of the house and the sand underneath.

The new township of Dayak Gardens was right in front of the avenue of stilted houses. The jungle of tall grass, which was etched in my memory, was no longer there. The grass had given way to concrete.

I looked at Damla. She was explaining to the others about her house and the neighbourhood. She was all excited to be in familiar surroundings. She must have spent lovely times in this area. Who would not be excited to make a return to their childhood town?

Now we had to understand where exactly her origin was. Where would her parents have spent their earlier life before the birth of Damla? This was important. When we went around this area, I had to watch her carefully to understand whether her personality was going through any alterations.

I had already conveyed to Mansour the gist of what I had discussed with his grandfather on the phone yesterday. So he was aware of what he should be looking out for.

The major problem was in finding out from where the negativity had entered her soul. Her parents were from a good background and were well respected in Konya. After their return from Sarawak, they had settled down in Konya and had been moving well with the other residents of the city. So by genes, Damla should have inherited the good nature of her parents, which was true. But her inner personality had been developed by the negative charges which had got absorbed by her soul during her growth in Lutong.

From the visions I had, it seemed that Damla's parents had spent a long time in the Dayaks' area, which could be the Dayak Gardens. The now-extinct jungle could hold the key to the evolution of Damla's soul. Maybe Altaf could help us through his father and grandmother. That thought made me more confident. At last, there could be some source of knowledge which, as Mahmoud had told, could make Damla's soul fully positively charged.

I woke up from my reveries with the ring of my cell phone. It was Altaf. He was in front of the Dayak Gardens. I directed him through the phone, and finally we met each other.

He looked similar to his father in the photo which I had with me—a handsome young guy. Even though he was of Dayak origin, he gelled well with the other inhabitants of the city. I remembered Sari and the smell of bamboo which she used to have from living in huts made from bamboo. I used to like this smell a lot. I could clearly see Sari in my mind.

I introduced Altaf to the others and told them how I located him. All were very happy that I could meet my old connections.

I was not sure whether I saw a moment's change of face on Damla. Maybe I only thought of it, but it was as though she had seen somebody whom she knew and did not like. That peculiar look in her eyes just flashed by or maybe it was just my imagination since I had been always thinking of this.

We sauntered around the houses. I managed to fall behind with Mansour and Altaf. The others were fully rapt to what Damla was explaining about her childhood years.

In short, we explained to Altaf our purpose for coming to Lutong and the problems we had been facing with Damla. Altaf was surprised to hear our story of souls charged with positive and negative energies. It was all above what he could grasp with his education being in arts and English literature.

But Altaf ensured us that he would take us to his father and grandmother who could throw some light on the past of the Dayaks. Maybe they would know the history of Sera Seri and Salamah.

Altaf recollected the stories of evil spirits which his grandmother used to tell him when he was a child. What they used to term as *evil spirit* could be the negative energy, and the heroes in the stories are the carriers of positive energy.

So our next stop had to be Altaf's house. Altaf insisted on having lunch in his house. The children were excited to visit the house of Sari and to have a taste of the local dishes. Viv and Kav were always ready to savour any cuisine. Their policy was to try them at least once to understand different cultures. For them, knowing the culture of a nation is done through the stomach.

On the journey from Dayak Gardens to the house of Altaf, I went with Altaf in his car. The others followed, with Viv in the driver's seat as usual.

Within twenty minutes, we reached the house of Altaf, Ahmed, and Sari. They were all staying together. It was a modern house with no indication of the Dayak dynasty.

When we entered the living room, the first thing which caught my attention was a photo hanging on the wall—a very old photo of my parents and us children! I pointed this photo to the others.

'This is one of the most cherished photo for my father and grandmother. They have told me a lot about your parents.' Altaf was quick to comment on the photo. 'That small boy with a naughty look must be you, San.'

I nodded my head in agreement with Altaf. We had a similar photo in our house as well.

We took seats around. Then Ahmed Menser entered the room. After the greetings and shaking hands with everybody around, he introduced himself to all of us. He told us that his mother was sleeping and would wake up within about ten minutes. She was old, and he did not want to break her routine. Meanwhile, Altaf's mother served us fruit juice.

We were talking between us in small groups. As usual, Kav and Viv were with Damla, and Jai broke into a conversation with Altaf's mother. That left us four men together at one corner of the room.

Altaf made us understand that his grandmother could talk only a bit of English. When we meet her, he would interpret her words for us so that we can fully catch the meaning. This was very important for us since we intended to get maximum leverage from Sari's knowledge about the history of the Dayaks. We had to necessarily understand the reason for Damla's strange behaviour.

Then Ahmed stood up and asked us to follow him to Sari's room. We went with him in a line to enter the room adjacent to the living room.

There she was, my old Sari, sitting on the cot, waiting for us to come. They had already alerted her on her guests from the past. She was also equally happy to see me. When I went near her, she planted a kiss on my forehead.

Sari asked me in half English and half Malay, 'How are your parents? I had loved them so much.'

I knew how much my parents had cared for Sari. 'Both are no more in this world, Sari. My father left us in 2005, and mother expired in 2008. Both were in their early eighties when they had to leave us alone.'

Then it happened. Damla lunged at Sari with a loud scream. It seemed either Mansour had expected this to happen or he had rapid reflexes that he caught hold of Damla before she could reach Sari. I did not dare to think what could have happened if Mansour had not restrained Damla at the spur of the moment.

Mansour held her in a strong embrace and pacified her in Turkish. Slowly her temper cooled down, and she came back to her normal senses. Mansour guided her out of the room.

Sari's face was grave. But after some time, she broke into a wide grin, and she started saying *salamat* to all of us. Then Altaf's mother announced that lunch was ready.

I motioned for Viv to take all the others to lunch and to leave Altaf and me with Sari. Viv understood what I had in mind and did as he was told without asking any questions. After some time, Mansour also came in. He had left Damla with the others. She had calmed down and, as usual, had no memory of what had happened in Sari's room.

With the help of Altaf as translator, we started conversing with Sari.

CHAPTER 24

A Twist From Her Story

'The Dayaks have a long history dating back to centuries in this country. The earliest known clans had been ferocious cannibals. Later they were more tamed and left the habit of eating human flesh. But they still continued to be headhunters. The most chivalrous warrior was the man with the most number of heads to his credit. They used to shrink the rival's head and put it on large chains which adorned their body.

'As in any other tribes, there used to be people opposed to this ferocity of the warriors. So always there were two sides for anything, which also happened in the vicinity of the Dayak community.

'Maybe about 200 years back, they started to have their own witch doctors, who were also known as medicine men. These people would heal the sickness of others with their jungle medicines, and many had their own mumbo jumbo tricks to keep the frightened people obedient to them. After the chief of the tribe, the witch doctor was the most powerful person in the tribe.

'There were many stories of the chivalry and valour of the Dayaks, which had been passed on by word of mouth from generation to generation. It was always about the good winning over the evil. But which was good and which was evil depended on the narrator and on which side the narrator was. Thus, two strong factions of the tribe grew. They were opposed to each other but were living together. Nobody could trust another since they were not sure on which side they were.

'The sultan of Brunei had always tried to rule Sarawak from far off. Sometimes he succeeded, and sometimes he had to face grim opposition. He had lost many of his warriors in ambushes orchestrated by the Dayaks.

'The major portion of the Dayaks wanted to live in peace and was secretly assisting the sultan. But whoever fell prey to the eyes of the medicine men were killed without a second's hesitation. Therefore, the people were generally afraid to openly admit that they wanted the sultan to rule.

'However, with the advent of the white rajah in Sarawak, things started to change for the better. The sultan gave full powers to the Brookes, and they ruled with an iron hand over the medicine men and a soft heart for the good people. This helped the Dayaks to progress a lot in their lives. Their lifestyle started to change. But they were still living in the jungle in bamboo huts and thatched sheds.

'The rajah tried to keep the people together and give the Dayaks and other tribes equal rights all over the country. Many agreed to be with him, and even from the Dayaks, there were many who joined the rajah's army. Naturally, the black warriors with their medicine men loathed these people and plotted many reprisals.

'The sultan used to send his warriors to assist rajah's army, especially in the Miri area. As you might be aware, the rajah ruled from the capital city of Kuching, which is miles away from Miri. It was not always easy for him to control the governance of this area from a long distance. That is where the sultan helped him by sending his troops. There were stories of how the spies of the sultan killed many a strong medicine men of the Dayaks.

'As in every country, the folklores continued to travel around from person to person, glorifying the strong and the good. Everywhere children always liked to hear the good winning over the evil. In Sarawak, this was also true.

'Then the Shell Oil Company came and struck oil in Miri. You will see the Grand Old Lady on top of Canada Hill, which was the first well to produce the black gold.

'This event started the trend of changing the lives of the residents of Miri. Even then the jungles remained, and many Dayaks insisted on not leaving their bamboo huts in the jungle. But the British government, who had taken over from the white rajah dynasty, partly succeeded in the rehabilitation of the Dayaks from the jungle to the city.

'Once the State of Sarawak became a part of Malaysia, the Malaysian government moved in fast to transform the jungle into the present Dayak Gardens. Many of the Dayak families who preferred to have houses in their old habitat were provided with free housing or were compensated by way of money or houses in other areas. The government rightly wanted to mix the Dayaks with other tribes and ethnic groups so that all would be known as Malaysians in the end.'

When Sari stopped to drink water, I had to open my mouth. 'But how do all these affect Damla? In which way could she be connected with any of these events from the history of Miri?' I saw Mansour nodding his head as though he also wanted to ask the same question.

'That is part of the upbringing of any child. What is being filled in a child's mind has a great effect on its future life. During your infancy, you frame your opinion about the good and the evil. If somebody had told the child again and again that the medicine men from the Dayaks were the good people, the child's mind will take that as an accepted fact, and this will remain etched in its inner self.

'When the child grows up, it may see other things and change its outlook of the whole world. But the subconscious mind will always bear inclination towards the stories which it thinks were the truth. The same thing could have happened with Damla. Who were her parents, and where were they living in Miri?'

Mansour explained to Sari the life of Damla in Lutong, which he had learned from Damla.

'Who was her nursemaid during their stay in Lutong? Do you know that?'

I could not understand what Sari was getting at, but I knew she would be asking relevant questions only.

Mansour was trying to recollect the name of Damla's nursemaid. 'It was somebody with a surname like Seriatti, I think.'

'You are sure it was Seriatti?' Sari's voice was a little high, and it showed a sense of anxiety.

'Coming to think of it, I am sure it was Seriatti.' Mansour confirmed his knowledge on the subject at hand.

'Then that was the problem with Damla. The Seriattis are descendants of the woman witch doctor Sera Seri.'

That gave me a jolt. How did I get this name in my dream? The first vision I had yesterday was with the woman witch doctor Sera Seri being killed by the sultan's spy. My worst suspicions were going to be proved true.

Sari continued her narration, 'That is the root cause of the whole problem with Damla. The nursemaid, being a descendant of the witch doctor, would have filled her mind with stories glorifying them and denouncing the sultan and the rajah as the worst offenders of justice. The small child Damla had grown up hearing these types of stories. So naturally, her inner self would always be pining to be one of them.

'That is the main reason for why she behaved the way she reacted in seeing me. I am from the conservative part of the Dayaks, who had always been at loggerheads with the medicine men. We Dayaks believe that when you are convinced about something, your soul would smell the troublemakers or the sworn opposition.'

'What about her enmity towards me?' I asked Sari. 'I had always felt that at some particular moments that she had looked at me with a vengeance. Her eyes talk about the revenge she was lusting for.'

Sari had not shifted from her crossed-leg posture from the start of our conversation. She closed her eyes for some time as though in meditation. Even though she opened her eyes again and started to talk after a few seconds, for me it was like an eternity of suspense.

'San, you were born in Seria, which is a part of Brunei lying very close to Miri. The sultan used to send his troops to Miri in the olden days from Seria since that was the easiest access to the city. The main characters were always men from Seria, and they were killing the evil men and women from the Dayaks like Sera Seri. So logically, the soul of Damla would loathe the soul of San. Both had been in opposition from centuries. It is quite natural, if you think only about the inner self. Where were you all when Damla went violent after coming to Miri?'

Mansour answered to that query, 'We were returning from Seria and had almost reached the outskirts of Lutong when she screamed and jumped out of the car. If I recall correctly, we were close to that large pond on the western side of Dayak Gardens.'

'The pond—that's it. The pond has a long history in itself. The pond is very old. You can say that it is almost like an ancient relic. It was there from the times of my great-great-grandfather.

It is told that the pond was the area where the cannibals used to throw the dead bodies of their preys and where the headhunters used to throw the cadavers after beheading them.

'But the major problem came up during the raid conducted by the sultan's army. Many of the followers of the medicine men were slaughtered and thrown into this very pond. It is rumoured that even the body of Sera Seri was not given a proper burial and was left in the pond. These stories made people afraid of this area in the olden days. The common men believed that the souls of all these people wandered around this area.

'Damla's nursemaid would have told these stories to her, and she, being born and brought up in Miri, would have known the pond very well. It would have been just the psychic effect of seeing the pond and remembering the old negative stories from her nursemaid which would have made her act violently.

'San, the western side of the Dayak Gardens was the main dwelling area of the medicine men when it was full of green jungle. Our ancestors used to occupy the eastern side of the jungle. That was the abode of conservative, peace-loving people.

'I would suggest that you take Damla to the eastern side of the Gardens and keep walking around that place. Let her get infused with the positivity from that area for a while, which will help her to forget the negative effects from her nursemaid.

'You should go there during sunrise. At dawn, the darkness gives way to brightness. That is when the light emanating from the sun overpowers the negative effects of the dark. The effect of souls are said to be at its best during this time. Let us hope for the best for Damla.

'I can see how concerned Mansour is for Damla. They should make a lovely pair. I wish them a very long life, and I am sure my wishes will come true.

'San, now you should have lunch. Before you leave Miri, please do drop in again. I still remember the naughty boy sliding under the stilts of the house, giving headaches to his mother. My salamat to your parents. I am sure they will receive it, sitting high above us in heaven.'

I kissed her hand and retreated from the room. Altaf had indicated to us that it was time for his grandmother to have her afternoon siesta.

We had our lunch in silence. Each must have been brooding over the history as told by Sari and the twist from her story.

Sari used to tell lots of stories during our childhood—tales from Malaysian folklores and the history of the Dayaks. The characters from her narrations had been hiding inside me, and now I could relate many of them to my dreams. What were in the realm of oblivion were coming out to the conscious mind, starting with my dreams on spinning. The theory of spinning had a cascading effect.

I used to always like the stories of Abdul Rahman, the clever spy who eliminated the dangerous Sera Seri, and Abdul Lahiri, the master of the warriors of the Loyal Ring, who killed the notorious Salamah. I remembered how many times I used to make her repeat these two stories.

No wonder when my mind was in turmoil, these stories, which had been lying dormant inside my subconscious mind, had resurfaced. The familiar background of my childhood created the right atmosphere for me to screen the favourite stories in my brain.

Now there was some logical reason behind what was happening. But I could not forget the look of utter vengeance in the eyes of Damla when she was staring at me near the pond. I should get some explanation for that behaviour also. Otherwise how could we go back with a peaceful mind?

Mahmoud had talked about souls and their negative and positive energies. Sari had also touched upon the souls emanating positivity and negativity. So there must be something connected to the souls in what we were experiencing at present. We had to ensure that we were taking the right path.

Sari had talked about staying in the eastern side of Dayak Gardens in the twilight. It sounded similar to Mahmoud advising us to get recharged by going to our origins.

Then a thought struck me—if the dawn can bring positivity on the eastern side of the Dayak Gardens, the dusk could bring a load of negativity at the western side near the pond. A sudden chill ran through me.

When we were returning from Seria, it was near the pond that Damla broke into a run, and it was almost sunset. What would have been in her mind at that time? Was she planning to get refilled with the charges from Sera Seri? The time and place would have brought her back to the teachings of her Seriatti nursemaid!

I had to talk to Mansour urgently. We had to ensure that Damla does not go anywhere near the Dayak Gardens till tomorrow morning.

Even though the twist from Sari's narrations made it all look like effects of our childhood learning, she had also warned us by touching on the subject of the souls getting refreshed. That was a cue for us to be alert.

'Let us go back.' Viv's voice brought me back to the present. All others were ready to move and had started saying farewell to Altaf's family.

When we were getting into our vehicle, Altaf came near me to shake hands with me. 'San, if you need any help you want at any time, do not hesitate to call me. I will be always there to do whatever is possible from my side. You have my number. Just say it is urgent, and I will be with you.'

I thanked him for the offer of assistance. Even when I told him that everything should go well from now on, somebody from inside me was urging me not to be complacent.

CHAPTER 25

Dusk to Dawn

We returned to the hotel. We had not firmed up our plan for our return trip to our home countries. So we decided to meet around five in the evening at the lobby to talk about a new itinerary.

That left us with an hour of relaxation. But I could not relax the way others were doing. My mind was in a quandary since we were yet to solve the issue of Damla's dual personality. I was hopeful that as suggested by Sari, if we go to the eastern end of Dayak Gardens during dawn, she should get cured. But how could we convince her that we should go to that area so early in the morning? She should not feel suspicious. An iota of doubt, and she would vanish from our hold.

Viv had set the alarm for 5 p.m. I was jolted from my stream of thoughts with the alarm going off at the right time. All got up from their slumber, and we trooped down to the restaurant.

Mansour and Damla were already there. With Damla's behaviour high on his mind, Mansour would not have been able to sleep or even relax. That was why they were already in the restaurant.

All of us ordered coffee with sandwiches.

While eating the sandwiches, we talked about our return journey. We had to take a flight to Singapore, which available in the morning every day. Mansour and Damla had to catch the Istanbul flight from Singapore, and they decided to leave with us in the same flight as we were taking the flight on the day after the next day. So we had a full day available with us.

'I want to see a sunrise of Malaysia.' I had to start the subject.

Viv picked up the conversation. 'The east side of the Gardens has a river flowing, and the land beyond the river is plain land without any tall trees. I think we should be able to see the rising sun on that side. But we have to wake up quite early for that.'

'Why not?' That was Kav. 'We have been relaxing all these days. So why not rise early for a good cause?'

When Kav said yes, her friend Damla went along with her. That was what I was hoping for. So without any fuss, we planned our itinerary so as to be on the eastern side of Dayak Gardens at dawn. At least the first step of Sari's advice would get fulfilled. After that, somehow I had to take them again to Sari to check whether she would get the same shocking behaviour as before. That was the only way to test the effect of the entry of positive energy into Damla's soul.

By the time we finished our discussions and the coffee, it was almost six. The sun was still up and was just going down on the west.

The girls and Viv wanted to go shopping at the mall. Since it was next door, Jai also went with them. Mansour and myself excused ourselves by stating that we had to rebook the tickets through the travel desk at the hotel. We wanted to be away from them so that we could take stock of the situation and decide on the final steps to bring Damla back to normalcy.

I could feel the concern Mansour had for Damla. He confessed that over the past few days he had become madly in love with her and that the moment they return to Konya, he would ask for the permission of his parents to fix the marriage with Damla. So it became all the more important for us to bring Damla back to her normal senses.

'Mansour, I had wanted to ask you about what had stalled you in Konya before coming to Miri. But I never got a chance to start this conversation with you since Damla was always around you.'

'I too wanted to tell you, San. You remember that I told you about her going to her parents' hometown? That was what she had told me. However, when she came back, she was behaving very strangely. One time when we were having coffee in that same Coffee House where we met her for the first time, she broke into a ferocious tantrum. I restrained her with great difficulty.'

'But what could be the reason? Did anything untoward happen at that time?'

'Nothing specific that I could note. We were discussing about our trip to Miri and meeting you here.'

'Then it could have been the mention of Miri and me together that triggered the enmity switch in her mind.'

'Coming to think of it, after going through the incidents that had happened here, I would say what you said is correct. San, Miri and Damla do not go well together. As Sari was saying, it is all mired in the history of this place and the wrong upbringing of her by the Seriatti nursemaid.'

'Mansour, I think she did not go to her hometown. I strongly feel she went back to Dubai. I had seen her during our return from Dubai on the trip we made when Jai and Kav had come for their visas to Oman. While crossing the sand dunes, I had seen her in the shop where the drivers usually stopped us before going on the dune-bashing. She was looking towards the road, and I saw her face clearly. That was why I had called you to check where she was, but you had replied that she had gone to her hometown. I left the subject there, thinking I had made a mistake and did not give much thought to it.'

'But why did she go there and lie to us?'

'Think of it this way. Her soul's sworn enemy is my soul. There is no personal enmity otherwise. Only the negative part of her soul had been searching for revenge. It could have been a mysterious manipulation or an unintentional coincidence that she met us in the Dubai desert camp. She must have decided that her way to me would be through you, and luckily for her, we had become friends in order to pursue the cause of those shapeless entities I had seen next to you.'

Mansour followed my logic correctly. 'She found a way to meet us in Konya and see how well she could lure you all the way to Miri, her birthplace, where she will be in her strongest to achieve her goal.'

'You are right, Mansour. I think she must have been misled by those negativities which had haunted you in the deserts of Dubai. That is why she went again to Dubai without telling you. Even though Newton's law of attraction states that the positive pole attracts the negative pole, here the negative soul is hungry for more negativity.'

'That gives us a fair idea about the sequence of events which had pulled the three of us together. Even though the causes were not all that auspicious, I hope that the results would be good for all of us. I love her, San, and I am determined to marry her. I am very confident that she will change herself to be a good girl for me. Of course, I require your full support to make her shed her dual personality.'

We had been so engrossed in our conversation that we never realized what the time was until we saw Jai, Viv, and Kav coming through the front door. When they reached us, we realized that Damla was not with them.

'Kav, where is Damla? She was with you when you went shopping.' I was really concerned.

'She left us, saying that she had a headache and wanted to relax in her room. That was about a couple of hours before,' Kav replied.

'But she never came to this side.' That was Mansour. 'Let me check in the room and give her some aspirin. She would have gone by the backside elevator.' Mansour went towards the elevator area.

Jai, Viv, and Kav went to our room, saying that they already had food from the mall's food court, so they did not want to go for dinner. I bade them goodnight and continued to sit at the lobby, waiting for Mansour.

I looked at the watch and saw that it was already 9 p.m. An overwhelming panic gripped me. My mind was racing. It was nine now, and Damla had left them two hours back. That means around seven, and that was just the sunset time—the dusk. Did she go to her room or to the western side of the Gardens to the pond?

I got up from the chair and was about to call Mansour when he came barging from the elevator. 'She is not in the room.'

'Let us get a cab and go to the pond, Mansour. I think she had tricked us and had gone to get her negativity strengthened for a final assault on us.'

We rushed out and took a cab from the front gate of the hotel. In fifteen minutes, we were at the Dayak Gardens. After paying off the cab, we ran towards the pond.

There she was, sitting on the long bench near the pond. She looked at us, but her eyes did not show any signs of recognition. Our anxiety rose. Mansour went near her and started to talk to her. She kept a blank face without answering Mansour.

We sat beside her.

All of a sudden, Damla got up and started to swirl. She was spinning just the way the Sufis used to do in Konya. Her hands were spread apart, and she was spinning from right to left.

We were dumbstruck, seeing this action from Damla. I realized that she was trying to reach the souls, and it could be that she had been doing this from the time she went missing from the shopping mall.

Spinning during the sunset would have given her a lot of energy. But she would have absorbed only negative energy, and that was what her soul wanted to. I shouted at Mansour to stop her from swirling like this.

Mansour went near her and tried to hold her still. But with one kick, she sent Mansour sprawling down.

I got up to catch her from swirling away. But she was far stronger than I had thought her to be. Before I realized it, she pushed me down. I fell on the sloping bank of the pond and started to roll down. All I could hold on to was the sand around me. That did not stop me from plunging into the water.

In minutes, I was inside the pond. I saw Damla rushing down. I tried to get up, and that was when she stamped me on the head with her foot to push me further down in the water.

I was not a good swimmer, and even somebody who could swim would have drunk a lot of water with this type of unexpected assault from a lady.

Mansour came to my rescue just in time and pulled me out of the water. I got up with water dripping all around me. I thought of all those cadavers who had been thrown into the pond over the years, and I felt jittery. For all that matters, I could have been drinking cadaver juice.

'San, are you all right? Never thought she would do this to you.'

'Never mind. I am okay. But where is Damla? We have to take her back.'

We climbed out of the pond. But Damla was nowhere to be seen. She had vanished. Again, we panicked.

We had to find her. The area beyond the pond was thick with trees. We started our search from there. It was a residential area, and luckily, there were light poles at every glade in the thicket. That gave us enough light to find our way around.

I saw that the time was almost 11 p.m. It would become more difficult as time flies by. We had to bring her to the eastern side by dawn. It was the summer season, so the sun will rise almost around five in the morning. We had hardly six hours to get our plan in place.

We should get some help from somebody who knows this area. That reminded me of Altaf, and immediately I called him on his cell phone. Altaf never asked why or what, and in half an hour, he was with us near the pond.

We explained the turn of events to Altaf, and he joined us in the search. But there was no clue to the whereabouts of Damla.

'Altaf, are there any houses in this area belonging to the Seriattis?' I asked.

'Yes. There was one where that nursemaid and her children used to live. That was right in the middle of these thick trees. Let us find it.' At last Altaf gave us a lead to find Damla.

We went around searching, and finally, Altaf found the house. We could easily identify the house since the board at the gate announced 'House of Seriattis'.

But the house was entirely in darkness—no sound and no light. The gate was open. Damla could have left it open.

We went around the house. There was no chance of getting inside. The doors were all locked. Altaf was trying each of the windows to see whether we'd have any luck. Finally, he could lever out one of the windows. There were wooden rods used as the grill on the windows.

We could easily break a couple of the wooden rods to give enough space for us to squeeze ourselves in. Once inside, Altaf groped for the light switch. But I restrained him from putting on the light. That would wake the Seriattis and could make it harder to get hold of Damla.

We moved around in the dark. Soon we realized that there was nobody in the house. It looked like an abandoned house.

So where could have Damla gone? How could she have vanished so fast?

'San, be careful.' I heard the warning from Mansour and, at the same time, the sound of shuffling feet nearby. But before I realized what was happening, I took a blow to my head and fell down. There were running steps and creaking of wood.

Mansour and Altaf together propped me up. There was a bump on the back side of my head. It hurt but not too much.

'Are you okay, San?' That was Altaf.

I replied that I was perfect. 'Let us go after her. I think she had taken the stairs up to the terrace.'

We ran up the wooden steps leading to the terrace of the house. The creaking of the wooden steps filled the still night. At least the wood had come to our rescue, and that was our cue to Damla's presence.

'She is upstairs. I can smell her perfume. When she came near you, I could get the same smell.' Mansour showed his prowess in tracking down Damla like a police dog.

We reached the terrace. In the moonlight, we could see the silhouette of a person near the parapet wall.

'Damla!' Mansour called out. 'Why are you running away from me?'

'Do not come near me,' Damla replied. 'I will jump if you come. Please, Mansour, stay away from me. It has nothing to do with you. But it has everything to do with this man who pretends to be your friend.'

'Do you mean San?' Mansour's voice started to break.

'Yes.' Damla sounded very firm. It was maybe Sera Seri speaking, or was it Salamah? 'I want this man to come near me. But do not try any pranks with me, or I will jump.'

In her mind, I was Lahiri or Rehman.

I walked towards Damla and stood near the parapet wall a little away from her. She asked me to keep my hands behind me, locking them together, and to look away from her. I obeyed her with the hope that Mansour and Altaf would be fully alert to rush her in case she attempted to jump.

In my mind, I was trying to analyze her behaviour to understand what her next step would be. Of course, she would want to throw me into the pond, where the Seriattis' ancestors were lying dead. But here she could be trying to kill me by pushing me down from the terrace. Within that moment of realization, she pushed me from behind.

My reflexes worked better this time. Even though I fell forward, I caught hold of the top of the parapet and hung there suspended without getting any foothold anywhere. My friends were quicker than I thought they would be. Mansour had caught hold of Damla, and Altaf came to my rescue.

When Altaf pulled me up, I saw that Damla was holding on to Mansour like a child. She must have come out of her trance. We went down the stairs and opened the back door, which was latched from inside. Maybe Damla had entered through this door and then latched it. We would not know for sure.

As we walked towards Altaf's car, I was thinking of what our next move should be. I looked at my watch. It was closing in on 2 a.m. That leaves us three hours to dawn.

A thought struck me. Damla was swirling at the pond to attract her negative forces. Then if we could make her spin at dawn on the eastern side while looking at the sunrise, would it not make the positivity enter her in a fast and strong manner? Yes, that was what we should do.

I told Mansour that we should go to the hotel immediately. He was reluctant to go back. Mansour wanted to wait at the east for daybreak.

'Mansour, let us get some Sufi music from your collection and request for a cassette player from the hotel desk. At dawn, we should become semazens at the east. Let us spin and make Damla spin too so that she reaches out to the positive spirits of Miri to fill her soul to the brim. We should ensure that there is no void space left in her soul for any negativity to enter. Then she is all yours, Mansour.'

That convinced Mansour. He wanted his dear damsel back to normal. Altaf took us to the hotel. We waited in the car while Mansour went to fetch his Sufi music and the player. Damla was sleeping in the back seat. But to make sure that she did not run away, we had both doors locked. Mansour came back fast.

We went back to Dayak Gardens. We found a bench near the riverbank and sat on it. It was 2.30 a.m. We had to wait for another two hours and more to get the first rays of the sun. It had been a long night. But if we could achieve what we thought we could, then all these efforts would be so fruitful. I touched the lump on my head. That was a reminder to be careful always.

Damla was still sleeping. She would be really tired with the ordeal she had been through. We let her sleep to gain some strength to do the spinning while the sun basks us with its first rays.

I thought of my theory of spinning into oblivion. Yes, we would be doing exactly that—spin into oblivion. The oblivion—was it nothingness or the unknown?

We waited there for the dawn to arrive.

CHAPTER 26

Spinning to Freedom

We were seated at the transit lounge at the Changi International Airport. There was enough time for us to laze around before the boarding time.

We were waiting for the Kochi flight, and Mansour and Damla were waiting for their flight to Istanbul, from where they would take another flight to Konya. They would stay in Istanbul for a couple of days to enjoy themselves and go around that beautiful city which had a combination of modern architecture and the ancient styles.

All were in a cheerful mood. As they say, all is well which ends well. I was pondering over the events which took flight just because of my pursuit of my dreams.

It was nice that I could meet Sari after all these years and make friendship with her grandson, the energetic Altaf. He had helped us a lot to get us out of the problems we were facing. He was the puzzle master for our Dayak conundrum.

My visions regarding the warriors from Brunei and their encounters with the strong Dayak women were logically based on the stories narrated by Sari during my childhood. Similarly, Damla's mindset had developed through the teachings of her nursemaid. She was brought up a by a Seriatti, and her mind was filled up with the glorified stories of many negative characters. To that extent, everything could be explained with a reason.

But where I got stumped was the enmity she had carried in her brain for me, whom she had not met before. That was where the theory of evolution of souls explained by Mahmoud fit in. One had to believe and give due credit to Mahmoud for his clairvoyance. His advice had helped us come out of this ordeal unscathed.

The series of visions I had experienced in the cave and on the lady's frock in the park could be explained only with the reasoning that the souls have their negative and positive energies. I had seen many things which I had never even heard of. Maybe those events also were part of the stories Sari had fed me with in those days.

In Niah caves, I had ended my ordeal in the dream with a sword being stuck towards me. Maybe at some time in the past, the soul which had entered my spirit could have been terminated by the pointed edge of a sword by one of the rebellious Dayaks. Or was it a premonition of danger lurking round the corner?

With all this logic, still the connection between Damla and me could not be explained properly. For that matter, how did I encounter Mansour in the first place?

The serenity on the face of Damla when we were spinning on the banks of the river yesterday morning was something I would relish throughout the coming years. That gave ample satisfaction to our minds after going through all these difficulties.

The facial expression she carried ascertained the fact that she could get rid of the negativity she had earned from the west during the dusk by spinning at dawn in the east.

The wait for the dawn was so stressful. The tension was almost killing me. I was afraid that we would fall asleep since we were very tired from the events of the night. The relief that

I felt when the first rays of the sun were seen over the horizon could not be described.

Mansour was the first one to stand up. He tried to pull up Damla along with him, but she did not wake up. Then he put his hands around her and lifted her up on her feet. While I was wondering how he would make her spin, he used a long cloth (probably Damla's scarf), which he had in his hand, to tie Damla with him. Damla was in front, and behind her was Mansour.

The cassette player was switched on to fill the atmosphere with the haunting music of the Sufis. That reminded me of the semazens and their swirling dance. Meanwhile, Damla and Mansour had struck a pose like the *Titanic* couple.

Mansour slowly started to spin with Damla. After a few rounds, I could see that Damla had woken up. Initially, she struggled to wriggle herself free. But with the soothing voice of Mansour in her ear, she calmed down. Soon she was moving around in the same way as Mansour.

I could not restrain myself for long. I had always wanted to try out this swirling dance, so I joined them in spinning around. Since we were on sand, I didn't repeat the desert camp debacle. I could see that Altaf was also spinning along with us.

After some time, my head started to spin, and then I stopped my 'tryst' with the Sufi magic. Altaf too had stopped. But the couple in front of us went on dancing. They were the experts.

There were sounds of running steps behind me, and I turned to look at Jai, Viv, and Kav joining us. In the morning, when they did not find me in the room, they thought of joining us at the riverbank as we had planned the previous day.

They were curious to see the way Mansour and Damla were swirling. Kav and Viv joined them to dance with the music.

All that time, Mansour and Damla were indifferent to our presence. They were in a world of their own.

I was watching Damla's face. She had a trancelike stare before it changed to a lively expression. The beauty of her face got ignited multifold in the red light rays of the rising sun. Mansour too had a serene look, and his face emitted the happiness he had found in Damla.

Together they were spinning into oblivion. This time, they emerged victorious. Mansour had achieved his goal. Damla was back in her real sense, far away from the dream world of the Seriattis.

When the music came to an end, they too stopped their dance. That was when they realized that all of us were around them, enjoying their dance.

Mansour untied the scarf and set Damla free, literally as well as metaphorically.

Damla rushed to Kav and hugged her. I could feel that Damla did not remember many of the things which had happened yesterday. Now I could see the old Damla chatting cheerfully.

Altaf took leave of us. We agreed to meet him at his house after lunch. We had to bid Sari goodbye. That would be a test for Damla.

We spent some more time going up and down the riverbank. Then we were back in the hotel to freshen up and enjoy a much-earned breakfast.

The boarding announcement brought me back to the present. It was the flight to Istanbul. Mansour wanted to move to their gate, but Damla was engrossed in talking to Kav. So he had to abandon his desire to walk out of the lounge.

Mansour came and sat next to me. 'San, thanks a lot for the help. Without you, I could not have got my Damla back.'

'Don't mention it, Mansour. All her problems were because of me, and fortunately, we could together stave off the danger which emanated from that. That was something which we could achieve with the wisdom of your grandfather.'

'Come to think of it, I met Damla due to this turn of events. Now I am very happy.'

'Mansour, the way you swirled with Damla tied to you was wonderful. It was very thoughtful of you to have carried the cloth to tie her to you. Otherwise, in that particular state of mind, she would not have danced on her own.'

'This trip had taught me to think of the extremes and to always to have a backup plan. Otherwise, we would have perished midway.'

'That's right. Even after the sema you performed, I was sceptical till the time we visited Sari. My heart was almost in my mouth when Damla met Sari in the afternoon.'

'San, the cry of exclamation she made when she saw Sari! I thought all our efforts were wasted. But luckily, that was merely the sound of happiness. I was so much relieved when Damla hugged and kissed Sari and when Sari blessed her.'

'Yes. That was the ultimate test for Damla. Now we can rest assured that she is her normal self.'

'All of you should definitely come for our wedding. I will inform you of the date. Without you, we won't get married, okay?'

I assured Mansour that we would attend the grand event.

Then came the last announcement for boarding for Mansour and Damla's flight. They took leave of us and started towards their gate. We watched them till they walked out of our vision. Just before vanishing around the corner towards the aerobridge, Damla turned her head to look at us. I could catch the glint of a tacit smile on her face.

She had the scarf with which Mansour had tied her to himself for the dawn dance. She waved the scarf towards us and soon was away from our eyesight.

The smile on her face . . . something was bothering me, but I could not place it. What was it that I missed? No, I could not recollect.

Then the boarding for our flight was announced. Kav was pushing me to walk, and she started to chat with me. I lost track of my thoughts. I was walking into my oblivion.

BIBLIOGRAPHY

Noetic Science <www.scienceofthelostsymbol.com/Noetic-Science.html>.

Large Hadron Collider <www.stfc.ac.uk/646.aspx>.

Inception <https://en.wikipedia.org/wiki/Inception>.

Tanoura <www.aletadances.com/tannoura.html>.

Dervish <www.whirlingdervishes.org/whirlingdervishes.htm>.

Rumi <http://dervishesofrumi.wordpress.com/rumis-life/>.

Konya <www.investinkonya.com.tr/en/konya.asp?SayfaID=1>.

Miri [blog] <www.miriresortcity.com/blog/ian/lutong_town>.

Miri, Lutong <http://blog.sarawaktourism.com/2012/09/spend-day-at-lambir-hills-national-park.html>.

Sarawak <http://en.wikipedia.org/wiki/Sarawak>.

Seria, Brunei <http://bumisepi.com/?p=1270>.